THE REDEMPTIONER

NORTHAMTON COUNTY

1. PENNEBAKER MILL
2. PENNEBAKER FARM
   (HOME OF JOHN SPARE)
3. GERMANTOWN ROAD
   (DRIVEN BY RICHARD HOLT AND JOHN SPARE)
4. MAIN ROAD FROM PENNEBAKER MILL TO
   GERMANTOWN AND PHILADELPHIA
5. ROAD FROM READING TO PHILADELPHIA
6. CHURCH. (JOHN SPARE ATTENDED THIS CHURCH)
7. BETHLEHEM (RICHARD HOLT HEARD GOOD MUSIC HERE)
8. ROAD FROM WARWICK FORGE TO NORRINGTON
   AND PHILADELPHIA
9. WARWICK FORGE
10. BUCKS COUNTY (THE DOANES LIVED HERE)
11. SKIPPACK (BANE'S TAVERN WAS HERE)
12. THE RED LYON
13. A TAVERN CALLED "THE WAGGON"
14. "   "   "   "THE WHITE HORSE"
15. "   "   "   "THE BELL"
16. MORRIS'S (THE HOME OF JUDGE MORRIS)
17. THE N. E. BRANCH OF THE PERKIOMY
   (SCENE OF THE FLOOD)
18. THE PERKIOMY BOUNDARY OF THE
   PENNEBAKER FARM
19. THE STONE MOUNTAIN (NORTH SHELTER
   OF SPARE'S FARM)
20. HOVEL WHERE A POSSE
   SURPRISED JERRY FERRELL
   AND MOSES DOANE

BETHLEHEM
7

West Branch of Delaware

BUC
10

Upper
Saucon

20

19

2

18

Pine
Forge

Peel
Forge

THE BLACK HORSE

SCHUYLKILL

READING

BERKS COUNTY

9.
WARWICK
FORGE

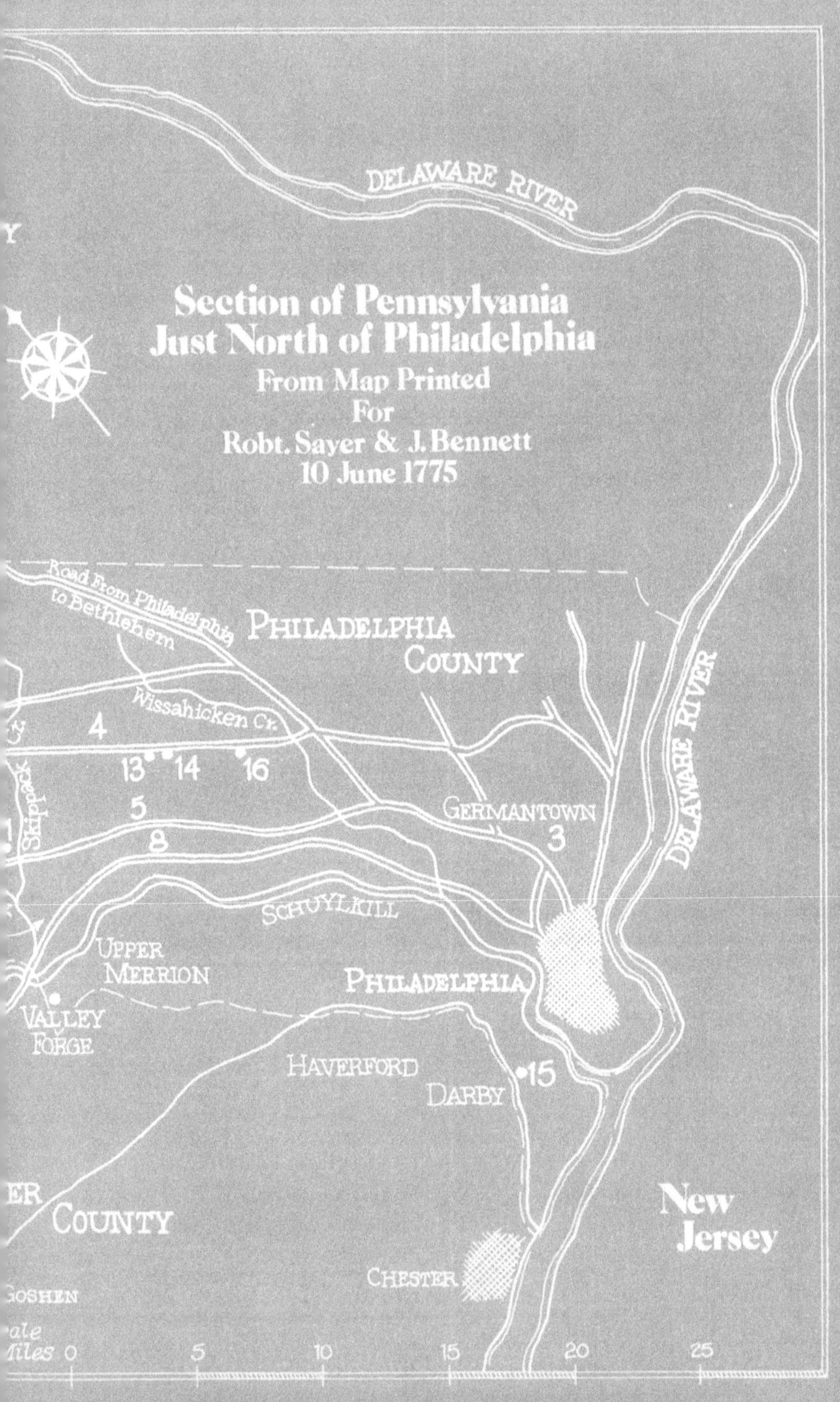

DELAWARE RIVER
Section of Pennsylvania
Just North of Philadelphia
From Map Printed
For
Robt. Sayer & J. Bennett
10 June 1775
Road From Philadelphia to Bethlehem
PHILADELPHIA COUNTY
Wissahicken Cr.
4
13 14 16
Skippack
5
8
GERMANTOWN
3
DELAWARE RIVER
SCHUYLKILL
UPPER MERRION
PHILADELPHIA
VALLEY FORGE
HAVERFORD
DARBY
15
CHESTER
New Jersey
ER COUNTY
GOSHEN
Scale
Miles 0   5   10   15   20   25

OTHER BOOKS BY
Isaac Rusling Pennypacker
Gettysburg and Other Poems
A Life of General Meade (1899)
Bridle Paths (1911)
The Valley Campaign (1911)
The Gettysburg Campaign (1913)
Quaker Origins (1927)
Meade in Command (1929)
Military Historians and History (1929)
The Valley Forge Burned by the British Troops, 1777 (1929)
Fort Beversrede and Beyond (1934)

THE REDEMPTIONER

BY

Isaac Rusling Pennypacker

Guilford, Connecticut

Published by Globe Pequot
An imprint of The Rowman & Littlefield Publishing Group, Inc.
4501 Forbes Boulevard, Suite 200, Lanham, Maryland 20706
www.rowman.com

Unit A, Whitacre Mews, 26-34 Stannary Street, London SE11 4AB

Distributed by NATIONAL BOOK NETWORK

British Library Cataloguing in Publication Information Available

Library of Congress Cataloging-in-Publication Data
The hardback edition of this book was previously cataloged by the Library of
Congress as follows:

ISBN 87106-113-9
Library of Congress Catalogue Card No. 75-151503

ISBN 87106-113-9 (cloth)
ISBN 978-1-4930-3313-3 (paper : alk. paper)
ISBN 978-1-4930-3314-0 (electronic)

∞™ The paper used in this publication meets the minimum requirements of
American National Standard for Information Sciences—Permanence of Paper for
Printed Library Materials, ANSI/NISO Z39.48-1992.

Printed in the United States of America

Contents

"Pennypacker's Mills" with "the barn larger than the house" that stands today across the Perkiomen Creek from Schwenksville, Pennsylvania.

A Note From the Publisher

WHEN THE MANUSCRIPT OF *The Redemptioner* was first
discovered it was accepted as a work of fiction from the fertile
brain of the late Isaac Rusling Pennypacker. Some careful
research, however, by Isaac's nephew, James A. Pennypacker,
revealed that Uncle Isaac had laid history quite accurately and
factually on grounds he knew well.

Early in the book you will find the young hero driving from
Philadelphia on "the Germantown Road" and from Germantown,
"Four hours later we came in sight of my master's home, and
cheerful and comfortable it looked. The house stood to the Eastward of the highway, well back from the road, and sheltered
on the North by higher ground, on which grew a grove of oak
and shell-bark hickory trees of large size. Westward sloped a
wide meadow to the shore of a creek. A field of Indian corn
seemed to me to resemble the camp tents of an army.

"The barn, which was larger than the house, was of a style
new to me, and I was told that it had been introduced by the
German Swiss."

There stands today "Pennypacker's Mills" across the Perkiomen Creek from Schwenksville, Pennsylvania, the German
Swiss barn larger than the house. But a short time by automobile,
were you to use horse and "waggon," and not beat the horse
to a froth, four hours would be just right for the trip. From
here to the end of the book you will find reference after reference:
"The Bell" tavern, the "Stone Mountain," "the grist mill on
the farm," "the flood on the branch," and many others.

Isaac Rusling Pennypacker set his story on the very farm that had been in the Pennypacker family since 1747 and is today owned by Margaret H. Pennypacker, the wife of the late Samuel Whitaker Pennypacker II. During Isaac's lifetime the farm was owned by Isaac's brother, Samuel Whitaker Pennypacker, who from 1903 to 1907 was the famous and somewhat controversial Governor of Pennsylvania.

The house itself was built in the 1720s by Hans Joest Heist, and in 1777 Washington made his headquarters there. In the original Samuel Pennypacker's own words, "on the 26th day of September, 1777, an army of 30,000 men, encamped in Skippack Township, burned all the fences, carried away all the fodder, hay, oats and wheat, and took their departure on the 8th day of October, 1777 . . ."

Today the house and barn still stand in a good Pennsylvania Dutch state of repair. Some of the land along the Perkiomen is now separate, and what is left of the grist mill, the fulling mill or the saw mill (it is difficult to determine which of the three remain) has been put to other use.

It does add much to this book to be able to trace this fictional story along the lanes, the roads, and the byways of fact.

The Pequot Press July, 1972

A Note From the Publisher

Two of the three mills of "Pennypacker's Mills" that stood on the banks of the Perkiomen Creek. The house and German Swiss barn are shown beyond.

THE REDEMPTIONER

1

Farewell to England

IN ALL THESE MATTERS, which I shall try to set down, it has ever seemed to me that I was a spectator, or an unwilling actor in a minor way, drawn on in spite of contrary plans and natural dislike for confusion and strife. My father, Philip Holt, had but a small landed estate, which went to my older brother, Robert. Our mother died three years before our father's death. My only possessions were a few hundred pounds, youth and a constitution that had warded off all illness from early childhood. From the cliffs, where the sea beat against the border of our English home, I could see the sails spread before the winds, which bore many a ship to America. For the turmoil of Europe, the fighting, or the talk of fighting on sea and land, I had little relish, and it seemed that there would never be an end of strife. With little schooling, I had learned from my father something of mathematics, the use of the surveyor's instrument and what else I could help myself to. In our neighborhood there was little work for a surveyor. I could draw a straight furrow, and in the corn lead all the reapers.

Our market town, where we sold our cattle and corn, was three miles away, by a road which was little better than the dirt roads that I came to know so well afterwards in America. In the quarter of the market town nearest our farm lived unruly people, much given to hard drinking, quarrels and unlawful deeds. If, when I was sent to the town by my father, I was detained until after the early autumn nightfall, I took the middle of the road for a mile beyond the town edge, and walked warily, with a tighter hold upon my stout staff. This caution was not entirely the outgrowth of the tales of misadventure, common enough in our neighbourhood.

After my mother's death, my father seemed less sturdy than before. My older brother, more and more, took over the direction of the farm, and it fell to me to do the selling in the town, and to collect the money due for the wool, sheep and calves disposed of. It was from such an errand that I was returning home one evening in April. There had been some difference of opinion between the cattle dealer and myself as to the accuracy of the account between us, and we had reckoned the amount of sales and payments again and again, until darkness came on, and I started homewards with sixty pounds in my belt. It was the hour of the evening meal, and the streets were almost deserted. In the poorer quarter of the town, where the disorderly portion of the people were housed, I encountered no one; but from behind the closed doors, now and then, came the sound of loud, sometimes, angry voices. By the time I had cleared the town, the new moon, in its first quarter, was darkened by rapidly spreading clouds, which soon hid the stars, even to the eastern horizon; and well as I knew the road, occasionally I stepped up to my ankles in some of the many mud holes which were well replenished every day by the frequent spring rains.

When more than a mile on my way, and just when a feeling of uneasiness, caused by the presence of the money in my belt, began to subside, I fancied I heard in the field behind the hedge a hardly drawn breath, as of a winded runner. Here, the road was but a narrow lane, and I knew that fifty yards further along was an opening in the hedge, an exit from the field to the highway. If any prowler had suspected the object of my visit to the cattle dealer, I felt that the hedge opening would be the place of danger.

Only a few Sundays before, father had stood Robert and me in turn, in our stocking feet, against the kitchen door-jamb; placed a book so that our heads, just touching it, could move freely under from side to side, and measured our heights. My brother was taller than I, but not so heavy. Neither of us had attained the height or weight of our father. My height was five feet, eleven and one half inches, and my weight, in my then twenty-second year, was 195 pounds or 14 stone, as we said in England. My mother had possessed unusual strength, and it was from her that I was supposed to have inherited my ability to do uncommon physical feats, such as the doubling up of a shilling piece between the thumb and forefinger, though some have doubted it until shown.

I had heard no other sounds from the field, but the ground was soft, and a prowler might be well ahead unheard. In the field, twenty yards from the hedge opening, was a familiar stony knoll, covered with trees, which seemed to increase the darkness of the dark night in the immediate vicinity. Walking as lightly as I could, but nevertheless every now and then striking a stone with my heavily soled boots, I had fairly passed the hedge opening, and had begun to think my uneasiness without warrant, when there was a rush from the roadside, which I heard rather than saw. Now, there was a deep ditch along the hedge, and this and the darkness helped me in a way that I had not looked for. My assailants—it turned out that there were two of them, of nearly my own size—became separated in their rush across the ditch, and afterwards the darkness helped me and hindered them. For I knew that any man in the road other than myself was an enemy, and as the footpads feared to speak, lest they make themselves known to me, one of them soon gave the other a blow on the head, intended for me, which laid his companion flat in the road. I was more than a match for my remaining opponent, and as soon as he saw this he took to his heels. Stumbling over the prostrate figure, I found that there was still breath in him, so I went home after father and brother Robert and a lanthorn. I was bleeding a little, and dizzy from a cudgel blow, so father told Robert to put the brown mare in our light farm wagon. We found the fellow still in the road where he had fallen, and father recognized him under the lanthorn, although his long hair lay across his face like a bloody rope. "It'll be Jim Ferrell, the rascal," said my father. We laid Jim in the waggon, and bore him to his mother who was a widow.

She was a sensible woman, and knowing Jim's habits, asked no questions when we had carried him into the house and laid him upon a bed. Jim Ferrell was a hulk of a fellow, who when he was on his feet, was recognizable at a distance by his lurching gait; and his way through life was as crooked as the lurch which he made from side to side with each footstep. He was harmless enough now for many a day, except for the trouble caused his mother.

We were busy at home, first with the hay, then with the corn and later with the turnips, and had no time to give thought to Jim Ferrell; but when the burden of storing the crops was over, my father and I undertook to fix the disputed line between our farm and the farm of Neighbor Stoneacre. Our neighbor was out with us, and we had been working for several days through a thickly grown hollow which was dry except after continued rain. The hollow broke downwards from a thicket on high ground in our front. Farmer Stoneacre had told us what his father and grandfather had said about the boundary line, and my father had told the Holt traditions, and we had come to a compromise in the afternoon and I had driven stakes along the boundary line agreed upon. This was on Wednesday afternoon. Thursday came with a heavy autumn fog, but we were out again early in the wet grass, and Neighbor Stoneacre was waiting for us. We expected to finish the work that day, but when we came to the spot where we had left off, we found that every peg for a distance of three hundred yards had been removed, and the peg holes filled so carefully that father and I would be forced to run the zigzag line over again. We had worked, with some intervals of talk, I judge an hour and a half in doing this, when from the thicket ahead of us came a mocking laugh. I put off in that direction as fast as I could run, thinking to find, perhaps, a pair of mischievous boys, and to award them proper correction. Ahead of me receded the sound of the trampling of bushes, now off to the left, and then to the right, so that I lost ground in the pursuit, but when I had cleared the thicket, I saw, disappearing through the fog, a blurred figure with a lurching movement which I thought belonged to Jim Ferrell, but I could not be certain. Not long afterwards we heard that he had disappeared from the village, and were well satisfied with the news.

In February following, our father died. I stayed at home until the second summer afterwards. By that time father's affairs had been settled. My brother, Robert, was in possession of the farm, and I of the few hundred pounds coming to me under father's will. I think most of the people who came over the seas to settle in America in the period that I did, or at any time in the first three quarters of the eighteenth century, were pressed forward by conditions at home, as I was, more than by any clear understanding of a promising outlook ahead. Having some skill in the use of tools, I made a stout chest, large enough for my needs. When it was finished, I thought that the month's work had been well expended. It was shapely, with an arched top, bound with iron bands; fitted with puzzle hasps, whose secret the uninitiated would require some time to discover; an ingenious lock, the key hole of which was approached through an apparently immovable cover; ample in size to hold sufficient clothing and some food for the voyage across the Atlantic, and painted a shade of green, like that of the American Maple leaves in the early spring. But the bit of handiwork that I was proudest of was a shallow, concealed space in the bottom, where, when I was ready to sail, I hid the coins that represented nearly all the value of my small inheritance.

All my preparations for the Atlantic voyage were completed a week before the vessel would sail, and I spent the interval in exchanging farewells with the friends of my youth, in visiting the haunts which were home, and in laying the doubts concerning my venture, which came over me oftener than I liked. Already I seemed to be widely separated from the flocks and the herds of our farm; and it was with a sense of remoteness that I gave the horses the last measure of oats, and threw down the hay for the cows. Even the old ram—there had been many a tussle between us—I began to regard with affection. Two days before the time set for the sailing, brother Robert took me and my chest in the cart to the harbor. On the morning of the second day, on a stretch of rough road, an axle broke, so that we did not arrive at the Bristol wharf until an hour before the sailing time. Already the tide was running out. On the wharf was much confusion. Boxes and chests, and there were still many of these to be got on the ship, were being put on board by the sailors. Many passengers already on the deck were casting home-sick looks ashore, and those on the shore were hurried on board by the ship's officers, in spite of the protestations of some, who wished to make sure that their chests were safely aboard first. These were told that their belongings would be looked after, and were not permitted to have their way. Robert and I placed my chest, as we were told to do, on the wharf, and I was directed to make haste as the ship would soon sail. Hurrying to the deck, I secured a place where I could shout a last word to Robert, and almost before I was aware of it the ship was under weigh, the sails being spread to a fair breeze, which with the ebbing tide was giving us a good start out of the port.

On deck was a pile of chests and boxes to be lowered into the hold. I stood by until the pile had disappeared, but saw nothing of my property. After an hour the mate, being at leisure by that time, passed where I stood, and when I addressed him respectfully, informed me that, owing to the crowded condition of the vessel, a number of chests had to be left behind, but would be brought to America on the next vessel that sailed, which caused me to wonder what I should do in the meantime.

2

A New Home

IT TURNED OUT that the ship owners cared little whether passengers paid for their passage or not. They had adopted a certain method of collecting the money due, after arriving at the port of destination. In the meantime they had the custody of the passenger, and that possession was sufficient security for the debt.

The voyage across the Atlantic was a weary one of three months' duration. The ship was overcrowded; the food bad, often unfit to eat, and the drinking water, if possible, worse. There was much sickness among the passengers and several deaths occurred. Ours was the common experience of people going out to settle in America, and I shall not dwell upon it, for to describe it would be to tell an old tale, which most persons have heard and many experienced. From these discomforts and this misery our minds leaped forward, like a bow from the released cord, when under a remote, blue sky, with a fair wind and a balmy atmosphere, which gave comfort to all, we entered the calmer waters of the Delaware bay, and began the ascent of the river, whose length seemed vast to me, familiar only with the shorter streams of England.

Some of the passengers had already paid their passage money. A number were to pay by the method with which I was soon to become familiar. I was alone in having started with sufficient funds, and in being deprived of their use, through no fault of my own. Yet I feared to reveal to the captain or mate the whereabouts of my hidden treasure, or to make any claim to lenient treatment on account of of it, and thought it safer to conform for the present to whatever fate the common practice had in store for me.

On the forenoon of the Nineteenth day of October, in the year 1774, our ship was made fast to a fragile, wooden wharf on the river front of the city of Philadelphia. From the hold the chests and some other personal belongings of the passengers had again been piled on the deck, whence they were borne to the wharf; and soon all who were free to go, were ashore. Those of us who had not paid for our transportation were brought together by the mate, and led by him to a large room in a warehouse, where quickly gathered a little throng of men, some from the town, and others, I judged from their garb, from the country. Among the last was a wholesome looking man of middle life, whom I took for a farmer. He moved about, looking at the immigrants, and presently, walking directly towards me, asked me my name, where I was from and what my occupation had been. When I had answered, he said, looking at my surveyor's instrument, which I carried with me; "Why do you not sell that and pay for your passage?"

I told him that I had feared that I might not be able to get another in America soon, and thought the one I had might be useful.

"It will," he said, "Plenty of work for a surveyor in America! Land grant lines to run! New roads to be laid out! But you tell me you know how to do farm work. You can plow, and mow, and reap?"

"Ever since my boyhood."

"If I pay your passage money, will you be satisfied to repay me in labor on the farm?"

The plan suited me well. I had learned by this time that the custom was for immigrants without money to bind themselves to labor for the American paying for their passage, until the sum advanced was repaid. All around me now these contracts were being made. Any man who had a trade, a blacksmith, carpenter or tailor soon found a home and a chance to make a new start in life. But I thought that I should not care to live with some of the Americans who were taking this means to get help. Some of them had a crafty look. Some were dirty. A few showed signs of being drunkards. The talk of others was coarse or vulgar. The American who had addressed me was very different from these. I watched him narrowly, liking his robust appearance and, above all, the sound of his voice, which all my life I have found to be a good indication of a man's habit and condition... Promptly enough, I accepted the offer made. My employer told me that there were some legal forms to be observed, a contract to be signed, according to which he would furnish me with a home, fare and clothing for a period of two years, while I should serve him faithfully for the same length of time. A record of this contract was made in a book kept at the Mayor's office, a precaution taken by the city rulers for the protection of the Redemptioners, as we immigrants, who bound ourselves out in this way were called, and also for the safe-guarding of the masters, who needed protection as much as those who served them needed it. There were those who were idle and vicious among the Redemptioners, and some of these I learned would get rid of the debt to their masters by running away to Maryland or New Jersey, after a few weeks of service.

My master's name was the short and simple one, John Spare. He informed me that we would not go to his home until the next day, as he had other business to attend to, and after he had taken me to the farmer's tavern on Third Street, whose inn yard, covered sheds and galleries reminded me of an English inn, he told me that I was at liberty to amuse myself for the rest of the day. After the long confinement on shipboard I was indeed glad of a chance to ease my limbs by a walk about the considerable city, which I was told then numbered nearly thirty thousand inhabitants, and was the most important in America. But towns and cities are all much alike to me—houses, shops and people—some with more and some less, so I left the town behind me, and finding a sheltered place on the river bank, stripped and bathed in the cool waters of the stream. That night I shared my master's bed, and was pleased because he knelt by the bedside and said a silent prayer.

We had breakfast by candle light the next morning, and my master's pair of sleek horses, already putting on their winter coats, were soon drawing us out of the city.

"This," he said, "is the Germantown Road," and soon we were in the village of Germantown. Here lived a printer of books named Sower, with whom my master was well acquainted.

"Christopher," said he, "this is Richard Holt, who is to live with me. His chest was left behind in England, and is to be sent to him on the next vessel. Will you get it and take care of it for him?"

Sower, a benevolent man, who made a practice of caring for the interests of persons living in the back country, readily promised to do so, and we went our way. Four hours later we came in sight of my master's home, and cheerful and comfortable it looked. The house stood to the Eastward of the highway, well back from the road, and was sheltered on the North by higher ground, on which grew a grove of oak and shell-bark hickory trees of large size. Westward sloped a wide meadow to the shore of a creek. A field of Indian corn, a plant which I had never seen before that day, seemed to me to resemble the camp tents of an army, for the corn had been already cut, and the stalks, bound together, stood upright in long rows, reaching the whole length of the field. There were two well covered fields of winter wheat, showing a deep green color. The barn, which was larger than the house, was of a style new to me, and I was told had been introduced by the German Swiss.

For a house I have never cared much, except as a place of shelter in the worst weather, or as an eating and a sleeping place. Nor do I care even now, and I cared still less in my young manhood for the things which clutter up a house. A table to eat from or to write upon, chairs to sit upon, beds to sleep in are convenient, perhaps necessary comforts. The rest I could do without. A barn is different. In it is nothing that does not pertain to the business of a barn. The living things which it shelters are seldom there when it is fit to be out of doors. The air of a house is disquieting. The barn is restful, and I never enter a well–filled barn without a sense of pleasure. The smell of the mows is a delight, and the sound made by fifty or sixty cows, as they pull mouthfuls of hay from the mangers and crunch their food, is music worth hearing; and I have heard some good music, too, especially at Bethlehem. Even the sight of so substantial and spacious a shelter for crops and animals, indicating a fertile soil and thrifty husbandman, was comforting and assuring. Also, I admit, the bright October sun rays, reflected from the window panes of the farm house, gave a feeling of warmth and cheer. I had fallen upon a cosy corner of the world, which except for the abundance of woods, did not give that effect of a new world that I had looked for, but seemed already long established, in the care of generations of men.

By the letter of the contract John Spare was master, and I was servant. In England, that relation would have been maintained. Here, I soon discovered, men stood more upon their merit and less upon their worldly condition. John Spare I found to be a just man and sagacious, but not hard. He could be master, when he chose, over men without help other than the manifestation of a quiet power; but in the two years that I served him, he never directly reminded me of my humble position, and only once, and then in an important matter, did he suggest to me that I was not his equal.

We went together to the cornfield in the early morning, husked the corn all day, side by side, at which work I was not his equal at first, and we returned before dark to feed, and bed the horses and cows. At meal time he sat at the head of the table, and I near the foot. Next to him sat his daughter, Eunice; and it was pleasant to see their bearing, one toward another. My master was a widower. Opposite him sat his sister, Mercy Spare, a single woman of nearly fifty years, I judged, much given to talking of persons and small things—a managing person, who liked to change the ways of people. In her I could see little resemblance to her brother, either in appearance or character. There were two boys, John Spare the younger and Charles Spare, the former aged about fifteen years and the latter twelve. Eunice, I thought to be eighteen or nineteen, perhaps. My master would have talked of England, and of the troubles brewing between the mother country and the colonies, but Mercy Spare's thoughts, like barn pigeons, took but short flights, and soon were hovering about home matters again. She had a persistence in this, I soon found out, that there was no standing out against. My master, as I came to know him better, proved to be a good listener but was no great talker, and during my first week in this American home he seemed to listen more to the cheerful unwisdom of the youthful Eunice than to the sage remarks of his sister.

There was on the table that evening a bread that was new to me, made of the meal of the Indian corn, and it had been baked in different shapes. Eunice Spare turned to me with a merry look and said, "Richard Holt, you have taken the wrong bread. That dent is my thumbmark, made in the batter to show father that it has no salt in it, which is the way he likes it."

While I answered that having tried the unsalted bread, I should now like to taste the salted, I was thinking of her form of address to me, and that she had quickly arrived at a considerate method. To have called me Richard would have indicated that she bore my position as a servant in mind. To have given me the title by which young women address a new male acquaintance would have been to ignore the truth. So she called me Richard Holt at once, and long afterwards. I was pleased to be called Richard Holt by my master's daughter, and was thinking of it when my thought was interrupted by Mercy Spare's saying across the table:

"Brother John! There is trouble at the tavern again."

"What now, Sister?"

"Two men from the city rode from farm to farm today, searching for another cattle dealer, who has disappeared. This one has been traced up the valley for thirty miles, and back again as far as this neighborhood. Here the trail stops, and nothing has been heard of the man for nearly three weeks. He had money. So had the other. Both trails stopped somewhere around here, and not a sign of the men has been seen since."

The two boys were listening eagerly, with a startled look upon their faces, but their astonishment could hardly be greater than mine to learn so quickly that crime had crossed the ocean to a vale, where I had hoped to find only peace and order. A disapproving glance passed from brother to sister, because, I supposed, of the presence of the boys, and nothing more was said on the subject until the lads had gone to their bed-room, which was next to mine, and where, later, I heard them talking in those whispers that carry so clearly, until they heard me in the adjoining room, when I hoped, reassured by my nearness, they fell asleep. At least they grew quiet. In the room below, after the boys had taken their candle and said, "Good Night," Mercy Spare returned to the subject of the missing cattle dealers, speaking with contempt of what had been left undone, and in a rising voice with indignation, of what she thought should be done to unravel the mystery of the disappearance.

"What would you have, Sister Mercy?" said my master, with a shade of annoyance in his tone. "That tavern keeper, Bane, has a bad reputation, but he cannot be put in gaol for two murders, when nobody knows that one has been committed."

"Well, if I were a man, I should do something," she replied."

"I thought the men who were making search, were doing something," my master suggested, whereupon, with her head held high, she called her niece, Eunice, and they went up stairs.

"Richard," said my master presently, "I am more concerned about these disappearances than I would have my sister and daughter know. Bane, the landlord, is a ferretlike creature, who grew up a few miles from here, and stories to his disadvantage have followed him from his youth up. There has lately come into his employ as hostler, a stranger, an ill-favored fellow, whose looks I do not like. Besides, there are stories that the Doanes in the next county have been pushing farther from home, and making the roads unsafe for market men. I am well pleased to have another able–bodied man on the farm."

❧ 3 ❧

At the Church Door

THE DAY was just breaking when my master called me the next morning. We were off early to the corn field, and spent that and many succeeding days in husking corn. Being new to it, I was awkward at the work at first, and the husks cut my hands until they bled. But soon I became as expert as my master, and before all the crop was hauled to the cribs, I could work as rapidly as he, and felt a little proud of it, especially when he commended me at the table before his sister and daughter.

I do not know whether it was the sea voyage, the memory of the indifferent fare on board the ship, or the change of climate and surroundings that made so welcome the sound of the horn which Eunice Holt blew to call us from the field or the barn to dinner and supper. Nor can I say that I ever ate, except perhaps on Christmas Day, as much as I could have eaten, being modest about my capacity before my master's daughter, in spite of what I have noticed, that women like to see the food which they have prepared eaten heartily of by the men for whom they prepare it. When I myself have put seven or eight ears of yellow corn, or four or five quarts of oats, in the feed boxes for the horses, I like to stand a while and see them enjoy the food, which I have helped to plant and store for them. By the time the corn was husked, cold weather had set in, a severer cold than I had ever known in our southern England. On the barn floor my master and I kept warm, threshing the wheat with flails, and at the work I was as good a man as he from the start, for I had learned at home. The threshing took us well into the winter before the bins were full of wheat, one of the mows and the overchute full of straw, and the barn yard deep in chaff. Long before the threshing was finished, about the time of our first winter weather, there was the butchering of the hogs, which, after the killing and distressful squealing were over, turned into a kind of merrymaking, with several of the humbler folk, men and women from the surrounding country to help. There were thirty–two fat porkers, and after I had learned about some of the dishes unfamiliar to me, but common in this country, I was ready to accept John Spare's opinion as to the profit of the pig as a domestic animal.

Two huge fires were built on the ground, and in these a number of stones were heated until some of them cracked. The hot stones were then dropped into vast cauldrons of water, thus brought to the boiling point, and by means of some active scraping and cleansing the bristles were released, and the whole carcass was made ready for the city market, or for cutting up into shoulders and hams for winter use.

Then came the careful smoking under a slow fire of hickory wood in the smoke house, and when that was underway, the grinding of the sausage meat, and the making of a dish called scrapple, either of which is very good on a sharp winter morning, and well carries a man through his morning work, especially if there come with it cakes made of buckwheat flour, baked on a griddle. Eunice was most skillful at making these cakes properly, and if the air in the kitchen was too hot, and the first buckwheat cakes were flat, and failed of being porous, it was Eunice who knew just how to correct the mistake, and she was proud to display her knowledge, too, which done, we all said something in her praise, when her color heightened very prettily. But the daintiest of all the dishes made from our fat porkers were the spare ribs, which to a hungry man were indeed a tid-bit, while they lasted. Sometimes, but not often, there was a cow to be killed, of which event word was sent to neighboring farm houses and portions were distributed among them.

This gave us an agreeable change to fresh beef for a while, and then we had a supply of corned beef, and with the latter a strange dish, introduced by the Germans, and called "Sauer Kraut," made by shredding cabbage very fine, and packing it tightly in a keg until its juices fermented, when it came out from the pot very delicate and tender. Now the odor of this dish while cooking was not appetizing, and it was difficult to keep the odor from permeating the house, and sometimes, with the wind in its favor, I have sniffed it clear to the barn, so that for some time I was not disposed to entrust myself to the dish. Often rallied on this point, I was persuaded one day to brave the danger, and as in some other matters, found the approach more terrifying than the reality.

On the Sunday following the talk about the missing cattle dealers, my master, his sister and daughter were to go to the church ten miles away, and I was to go with them. They were members of the church of England in America. John Spare was a faithful attendant at the morning service unless the roads were in a bad condition, as they often were at the breaking up of winter. Eunice Spare sang in the choir with a sweet soprano voice, and when she found that I had sung bass for a time in the choir in England, nothing would do but that I should do the same in America. The bay horses had been curried, and the large carriage washed on Saturday, and I thought the whole made a fine show as we drove in among the oak trees, which surrounded the church. Many of the worshippers had come on horse-back; others in vehicles. The sermon was a plain discourse on the harvest season. After the service, we in the choir of six persons followed the congregation out of doors where I saw John Spare and a group of men engaged in a conversation, which from their earnest faces I judged to be of serious import. So I waited until my master beckoned to me to join them. The most important appearing person in the group was a portly man of sixty years, clad in more costly garments than were worn by the others. To him all the others were listening, as if he spoke with authority. As I approached he turned to my master and asked: "Whom have we here, John?"

Addressing them all, my master said: "Neighbors, this is Richard Holt, who has lately come from England, and is making his home with me. We may confide in him. His youth will be of service in any plan we come to." The stout man, I learned, was Judge Morris of the court of the adjacent county, who was a warden of our church. His son, a man of my own years, was with him. The son's apparel, manner and way of speech reminded me of the young beaus I had seen on the streets on my only visit to London. The other men nodded, spoke or shook hands with me, but young Morris took no notice of me whatever, and when Eunice Spare came out of the church door, he moved away from us and joined her. My eyes followed him as he walked away, noticing his straight back and graceful carriage and the supple but muscular limbs, revealed by his small clothes. One of the older men of the group, a farmer from nearby, said to the Justice:

"Judge, your son, Theodore, wastes no time."

A shade of annoyance passed over the Judge's features, but he did not reply to the remark, resuming instead what he had been saying when my approach had interrupted him.

I did not catch more than the general drift of the conversation which followed, for I could not keep my eyes from the church door, where Eunice Spare stood, a pretty figure in the bright sunlight, listening to Theodore Morris. Every now and then her pleasant laughter came to me, and sometimes their voices took a higher pitch, but only occasionally did I understand a word, when with a severe effort I would fix my mind on what was said close by. In this fragmentary way I learned that the men had been consulting as to some plan looking to safety at home and on the highways. Judge Morris was saying in one of the intervals when I was not regarding the pair at the church door: "Now, men, you have nothing beyond a suspicion to take before the law officers of your own county, and that is not enough. Besides, your courts and Sheriff are in the City, and that is twenty-five miles away, too far for quick help. You would do well to meet at one of your homes, and hit upon some plan for mutual protection."

As many of the church goers had long rides before them ere they could reach their dinner tables, and Sunday was a feast day all over that part of the country, it was agreed not to delay longer in discussion now, but to meet at John Spare's house on the next Tuesday night, when there would be a full moon; and soon afterwards we drove homeward through a country bathed in the atmosphere of Sabbath repose, which seemed to extend to the pigeons, the chickens and calves gathered about the barns. We were quiet for the most part, even Mercy Spare succumbing to the influences of the day and the peaceful scene, but after we had gone above a mile her niece said:

"Father, Theodore Morris thinks these are wild stories that are going about the country, told to frighten old women."

"Which particular story, daughter, did he dispose of first?"

"He says each one is a part of a whole. He doesn't believe the Doanes are going to descend upon us, or that it isn't safe to go to the city market."

"No doubt the Morrises are safe. They are on the other side of the river. And besides, Theodore doesn't go to market. Yes, he is safe enough."

"What do you think, Father?"

"I told you that I thought the Morrises were safe."

"I heard that. But are we safe?"

"On this road? Yes, I think this road as far as I can see ahead, is perfectly safe."

"What about the other roads?"

"I can't see the other roads."

"Now, Father, you are teasing me, You know well enough what I mean."

"Well, daughter, if I hear of any real danger, I shall try to guard against it, and if I cannot meet it alone, we will ask Richard to help us."

And that was all his daughter could get from him.

That afternoon after dinner was over, and Mercy Spare had said that the hunger created by a long drive to church was some recompense for the journey, my master said to me that there was much small game about, quail, woodcock, hares and so on and that there were deer in the forest, back of the Stone Mountain. He proposed that we should put the guns in order, and brought forward a small arsenal of fire arms. There were two rifles, made by native armorers of wide repute. One of these rifles had two barrels, one set above the other. There were three shot guns and several pistols. All these were cleaned and oiled, and after melting the lead we made quite a store of bullets by the use of a mould. Mercy Spare came into the outer kitchen, where we had built a fire in the fireplace, and hoped we would put things back in their places when we had finished.

"Yes, Mercy," said her brother patiently.

"John Spare," she went on, "it's well enough for you to talk about shooting deer before Eunice, but you know you haven't shot a deer in twenty years."

"Maybe Richard Holt doesn't have any such scruples, Sister."

Whereupon she withdrew, as if she knew that it was useless to expect her brother to talk about something which he had on his mind, but was not ready to communicate.

❧ 4 ❧

Jerry by Candle Light

AN HOUR after supper time on Tuesday evening some of the men whom I had seen talking together at the church on the previous Sunday, came to John Spare's house, but only those who lived within a radius of six or seven miles. There was a keen air, and as the horses ridden were warm their riders led them into the stables of the barn. The men came by twos and threes, and in all there were nine or ten arrivals, the younger men coming on spirited animals, the older men preferring quieter mounts. As a general rule our American horses were not well broken, the training not beginning early enough, and the methods being too sudden and harsh. It was taken for granted that the purchaser would complete the breaking, and the consequence was that there were many horses, which otherwise would have been useful animals, that were of uncertain temper, and had the habit of running, kicking, shying or biting, and in some of them were combined several of these habits. So we had to stable the incoming horses with care, and it was done with considerable bustle of greetings, mingled with calls to the horses, the sharp sound of the shodden feet on the stones under the barn overchute and the slapping of hands on the animals if they hesitated to go into the stalls. This being over, we entered the house in a body, making a prodigious noise with voices and feet, and the scraping of the hickory chairs on the bare floor.

The women had put the room, which usually served both as a living and an eating room, in order, and on the table had placed some mugs of cider and what they called pies, made of the pumpkin. Though these pies had no top crust as an English pie has, they were so edible that a man could easily be persuaded to take a second helping. On the table, too, was a huge jar of yellow Maryland tobacco and a supply of common pipes. At first we went into the room opposite, which had a home made carpet on the floor, made of strips of rags, cut and sewed together in the evenings, and woven by a weaver of the neighborhood. But when Mercy and Eunice Spare invited us to the room where the pies and cider were set out, it was so much more comfortable that we remained there, and presently, when the women had withdrawn to their sewing, and the pies had been eaten, and each man had been provided with a mug of cider of a proper hardness, and those who wished it with tobacco and pipes, we were in a most cheerful mood, and I thought that the men had lost sight of the purpose of the gathering. For there ensued a story telling match, attended by bursts of laughter, especially when William Barnes, a merry fellow and a good mimic, told a tale or two. When I crossed the entry to fetch a couple of candles, I saw the two boys, who should have been in bed sound asleep, standing in their bare feet at the head of the stairs, clad only in their winter night drawers. I shook my head at them, whereupon they laughed at me and scampered off to their room.

I had just returned with the candles when one of the older men, Stacey Claypoole, asked:

"Where is Abel Strong?"

The young man, Barnes, answered that he had seen him the day before at Oliver's Mills and that he had declared it to be his purpose to be present without fail.

There was a general murmur of approval at this assurance, and I gathered that Able Strong's presence was desired, and that the rest had been waiting for him.

Claypoole remarked:

"Abel could easily have reached here in an hour and a half. He should have come three quarters of an hour ago. Let us go ahead and form some plan. We can hear what Abel thinks when he arrives."

There followed a kind of report, brought by the men assembled, of happenings and rumors in the widely scattered neighborhoods whence they came. Some of these tales all present had already heard. There was no new explanation of the disappearance of the cattle dealers. The extension by the members of the Doane family of their depredations into our neighborhood was known to all. But that a farmer from ten miles to the west, engaged in hauling iron from Warwick furnace to the city, on his return on Saturday had been waylaid when within a few miles of his home was news to all, except to the man, Boileau, who told the tale. Perhaps, because I saw some of these men, and heard of some of the occurrences now for the first time, the whole seemed to me more like a tale read in a book than like a reality. This impression of vagueness was increased by the remarks of the men present. No one of them had as yet any personal experience with troubles which they had come together to guard against, and what was said was more in the nature of comment than of suggestion of something to be done. Immediate contact with danger was lacking to give it substance. The men seemed to feel this, but did not give it recognition in any open way.

I asked William Barnes, who sat next to me, who the Doanes were and what they had done to arouse so much fear. His merry face grew grave for an instant as he replied:

"I hope you may never come to know them. They live in Bucks—a large family under the leadership of Moses Doane. The men are all powerful fellows, and for some slight they have taken to the highway, and in a few months their deeds have made their name a terror. Until lately they have not worked over this way, but a week ago a farmer was robbed on the road about ten miles up the valley, and the Doanes are suspected. If they are coming our way, the roads won't be safe."

My master talked little as the time went by, but at last, when it seemed that no plan of action was forthcoming, he said in his low voice, to which I found that groups of men invariably listened when he did speak:

"Well, neighbors, I don't see that we can do more now than for each man to warn the farmers in his own vicinity, and to recommend that on market days they travel in company as much as possible, and at all times when on the road carry fire-arms."

It was now nearly ten o'clock. Abel Strong had not arrived, and the company prepared to break up. John Spare and I walked with the men across the apple orchard, that was between the house and the barn. There was a well–trodden path across the orchard, plainly seen under the light of the full moon, and we followed this under the trees, over the knoll and down to the barn by the road side, the younger men ahead, the older men following, all somewhat silent, for the matter had been talked out, and the hour was late for country people. The saddles had been left on the horses and also the bridles, the bits only being dropped, and halters put on over the bridles, so the animals could comfort themselves with the hay in the mangers. Those ahead paused when the barn was reached, and we all gathered for a moment under the overchute. Out of politeness the younger men waited for their elders to bring out their horses first, but when George Heacock, Samuel Pearson and Job Tully, all of them under thirty years old, had entered the stable, we heard one voice after another exclaim:

"Why, where's my horse?"

"I put Beauty in this stall!"

"My horse isn't here."

"Mine was next to yours!"

The three best and most spirited horses were gone. Now nothing like this had ever happened before in the immediate neighborhood, they said, and at first all were struck dumb with astonishment, but as soon as it was clearly borne in upon us that the horses had been stolen, my master said:

"Some of you ride quick to the tavern, and see if they passed there!"

At once, four or five of us ran as many horses out of the stalls, jumped into the saddles and rode rapidly to the tavern on one of the two more direct roads leading to the city. The tavern lights were out, but a vigorous banging on the door, continued for some minutes, brought a half clad man, carrying a candle, to the door.

It was William Barnes, who had dismounted and thundered at the door. The rest sat on our horses in the road, I being somewhat in the shadow of a tree, which in the moonlight, I had time, before the tavern door was partly opened, to recognize as an Elm. From where I sat on my horse in the shadow, I could see fairly well the man at the door, for he held the candle high, and to my amazement there was turned towards me the face of Jim Ferrell, which I had last seen, livid and bloody, laid upon the cot in his mother's house, where my father and I had carried him after we had picked him up from the Somerset lane.

Had it not been for a long habit of not speaking on the spur of the moment, I should have exclaimed in astonishment now, but I said nothing. My second thought was that perhaps Jim had mended his ways, and if so, I would not give him a bad name. I could not hear Jim's replies to Barnes' questions, but was told that he answered readily enough, saying that all had just gone to bed at the tavern, and that no horsemen or led horses had passed that way towards the city. Barnes had him fetch a lanthorn, and I thought this showed no great degree of confidence in Jim Ferrell's truthfulness. Several of the men examined the road, but it was a highway much used, and nothing was to be discovered in that way. So we rode back to my master's. All was silent at the barn, but when we came to the house, we were met with news that, for the present, drove all thought of pursuit of the horse thieves out of our heads.

After we had started on our ride to the tavern, John Spare and the others who had remained behind lit the stable lanthorn to see if the thieves had left any signs behind them. In the stalls everything, except the halters, was as it should be. In the mangers the hay was half eaten. They remembered that the barn yard gate and the stable doors were properly closed when we had first reached the barn from the house. Next they explored the passage way between the stalls for the horses and the cow stalls. At the rear end of this passage way was a larger compartment, at that time not in use, but intended for calves. In this place they came upon the body of Abel Strong, and it appeared that the thieves had done for him, and thrown him where he would not be found at once. Arriving late Abel must have gone directly to the barn to put up his horse, and have come upon the thieves. If there had been a scuffle, there were no signs of it. More than likely they had knocked him senseless with one crack, and now he was lying on the spare room bed more dead than alive. Already George Heacock had ridden to Fatland, twelve miles away, for a doctor and until he came at daylight next day we were afraid almost to touch Able. In the meantime Mercy Spare put cool cloths to his head, though we men feared to draw off his boots because of the danger of dislocating possible broken bones. We passed a sleepless night, which I had never done before to my recollection. Long before day Eunice asked me to bring wood for the kitchen fire, and she prepared a substantial breakfast for all of us, I helping as well as I knew how. At some of my ignorances she laughed, and then said that it was a shame to laugh at such a dreadful time. At dawn the men departed, my master lending to all the men who had lost their horses, except George Heacock, who was off after the doctor, some heavy animals fit only for the plough; and mounted on these, with only horse blankets in place of saddles, they started homewards, needing no urging to spread the news as they went.

The doctor said, when he came, that Abel Strong's bones were not broken, that we might draw off his boots, and that he would stay until there was a change one way or another. The change came some hours later, and it was a change for the better, but we were told that Abel must not talk, so we were left with only our guesses as to what had occurred to Abel and how it had happened. It turned out when he was on the way to recovery that our guesses had been as good as Abel's knowledge, which in the darkness of the stable, had amounted to very little.

❧ 5 ❧

Choir Practice

Wherever the thieves and the stolen horses might be, the farm work had to go on. There were other matters which might not go on so readily. The members of the church choir were in the habit of meeting at the church on Friday evening of each week to try the hymns and chants. Now this had to be given up through fear of highwaymen, and it was agreed that we should meet at the church an hour and a half before the time of the Sunday morning service. In his mocking way Theodore Morris ridiculed the change, when he heard of it on the Sunday following the theft of the horses and the attack on Abel Strong. He did not sing himself, but often had ridden on his hunting horse to the Friday night choir meetings, and after the change was made was on hand very regularly at the early Sunday practices. I noticed that after the men arrived for the church service he had little to say on the subject, but previous to that time he seemed to consider my presence as no barrier to speech, and of Eunice Spare he asked questions, which in themselves were innocent enough but left a doubt behind them.

It was on the first Sunday morning when we had met to try the hymns for the day, while we were waiting for David Wilkinson and Annie Bates, who usually came together, to arrive, that I heard him say to Eunice Spare, a winning smile playing over his face the while:

"They tell me, Eunice, that there were twelve men in your father's house and some of them armed. How many robbers do they think there were?"

Theodore Morris and Eunice Spare had gone to the Church since their childhood, and they called each other by their Christian names. Eunice Spare had a ready wit, and was seldom taken by surprise, as I, myself, often am, or in want of an answer. At Theodore's question, it suddenly looked to me as if we had been at fault, even if our own voices had drowned any sounds from the barn, and the apple orchard and knoll of ground were between my master's house and the stable, and I had a passing wonderment as to why the dogs gave no warning that Friday night. Eunice quickly answered:

"Theodore, nobody knows how many robbers came to the barn, but I wish you had been at our house. Then, if there had been as many robbers as there were of our men, I am sure the thieves would have been caught."

She said this very sweetly, and if Theodore took any offence, he was not at liberty to show it. He said nothing more about the number of men that had been with us, but replied:

"Well, it wouldn't be worth while for your father to lock his stable doors now. The thieves are not likely to come hereabouts soon again, and when they were here they were after horses not choir singers."

There was revealed a hidden edge in the last remark, but I did not understand until afterwards why it should make any difference to him whether the choir met on Friday night or on Sunday morning. It was only gradually, as time went on, that I discovered the background to the opposing forces, which I had seen begin to play, one against the other, in the preliminary alignment of two hostile sides of a political controversy that was soon to terminate in war and the separation of her American colonies from England.

The Morrises, father and son, were of the old order. John Spare and the men who had gathered at his house, of the new. The times made strange alliances and as curious hostilities. Judge Morris from his position of honour and more than comfort in our world, I thought, did not look with favor upon his son's noticeable liking for the company of Eunice Spare, any more, as I found out afterwards, than John Spare could look with entire approval upon the love of a Redemptioner for his daughter. Theodore Morris's dislike of the abandonment of the Friday night choir practising appeared simple enough when I came to know the father's attitude. On Friday night Theodore Morris could see Eunice Spare, and the father know naught of his whereabouts. This pursuit on Sunday morning could not fail to be noticed, for the father was regular for a time in following to the meeting place.

I could not then conceive of conditions which would bring the Morrises and the robber Doanes upon any common ground. But, strange as it was, that happened in a measure, too, and from the extremes of their different worldly positions and by the most widely separated methods, it came about that both the Morrises and the Doanes were opposed to the men and measures supported by my master and his friends. Yet such was his virtue and integrity, that Judge Morris would have sentenced any of the Doanes, or all of them, upon conviction after a fair trial, to imprisonment or the hangman's rope. On the other hand, it is to be said of the Doanes, that if they had overtaken Judge Morris on the highway after dark, they would have robbed him with strict impartiality, and at other times some of them could wear stolen ruffles and, with the garb, take on the speech and bearing of the quality. For a long time I did not think that Judge Morris was just to Eunice Spare, or considered fairly the evidence of her beauty, her truthfulness and her wit. Of him, I said to myself, John Spare is a plain farmer without knowledge of the world outside of his own walk in life, and with no knowledge at all of the classics, a man of virtue and sound merit in his place, but one who has no silver or wine upon his table, or ruffles on his shirt, being clad instead in plain homespun, made from flax grown upon his own farm, and spun by his sister, Mercy, and his daughter, Eunice; a man who does not own a coach or have a coachman, but harnesses his own horses and litters his own cows, if need be.

It did not matter that Theodore Morris's devotions were not

paid to the father but to John Spare's daughter, Eunice, and that she was shielded from the harvest field, but she liked well to drive the loaded hay waggon from the field into the barn. Eunice Spare could make more pounds of butter to a gallon of cream than any farmer's wife for miles around, and she had a knack with the chickens in the spring, and the turkeys which were disposed to die off or wander away. After all, it must be admitted that she liked wholesome, simple things, and very likely, I thought, she would not feel at home at the great annual dance in the city attended by Theodore Morris and his sister, of which we young persons heard an account from the Judge's son one Sunday morning in February. I say that very likely she would not have felt at home there, but sometimes I thought that there was no proper walk of life in which she would not have felt at home, and which she would have even adorned, after a little trial. But I looked upward to Eunice Spare, and Judge Morris appeared to look downward upon her, and we saw different surfaces of the same object. At least that was how I settled it in my own mind.

Mercy Spare did not like the Sunday morning choir meetings any better than Theodore Morris liked them, and she let us all know her feelings in the matter. As at first she and her niece and her brother and I all went together in the carriage drawn by the two horses, it meant an early start, before she had time to see that the house was put in order and the dinner planned. By reason of this, and some fault of her own, she was seldom ready to start when I had driven the carriage to the door, where my master and his daughter were waiting. I never knew my master to be tardy, and tardiness in others caused him to manifest signs of impatience. With all her energy, and quickness of movement when actually under way, Mercy Spare, with or without a good excuse, was certain to be late. Ahead of her, time was an unlimited expanse, with no divisions allotted to different tasks, and when she had made all preparations to culminate in some performance, she would be diverted from the main purpose by a detail which had no bearing on her contemplated act, which was thereby deferred while she undertook some unimportant matter.

So after several Sundays of waiting for Mercy Spare to be ready, and of arriving late for choir practice, my master said that thereafter he would drive his sister to church in the gig, and that his daughter and I could make an earlier start on horseback.

When Mercy Spare heard of this arrangement she expressed approval, saying that now she would not have to listen to the singing of the same tunes twice in one morning. Later, when the roads were blocked with snow, she ceased going to church at all until the sleigh could be used, and in the interval John Spare went on horseback. Theodore Morris appeared as well pleased with the arrangement, which took Eunice Spare to the church ahead of his father, as Mercy Spare had been. On those first mornings, when we all went together to the church, and he understood that was to be our habit, he did not make his appearance until nearly church time, when he arrived with his father. As soon as he found that we had changed our ways, and that John and Mercy Spare remained at home, sending Eunice Spare and me on ahead, he was at the church in the early morning as promptly as we were, though his ride was five miles longer than ours and he had a river to ford. I soon saw how Theodore Morris regarded Eunice Spare. It took much longer to know how she regarded him. And it was a long time, at that period of life that is a matter of some months, before I felt that I would give up life itself for Eunice Spare's sake, and yet must keep my feelings to myself.

The tenor of our choir was David Wilkinson, a small, agile man above forty years old, and it was he who put the spirit into our singing. He would not let us dawdle over the church music, neither with the hymns nor the chants, as I have heard done in other churches in a manner which I came to dislike altogether, when I had learned from David Wilkinson the wholesome, heartier way. Nor did he let us make as much noise as we could with our voices, or gasp for breath in the wrong places, but regulated the volume of sound very delicately, according to the movement of the music. David on his way to church always stopped for Annie Bates, who sang alto. She was a year or two older than I, a plain little body with a kind heart, which led her to take notice of me when Theodore Morris under some pretence or other took Eunice Spare off to a corner of the church, and David, who was never satisfied with anything as it was, was fussing about the choir loft, the pews, or even the chancel when we were not singing.

As the winter wore on, and we heard of no more depredations, we felt secure again. The sleighing was for a time very good. When Christmas was drawing near we went back to the Friday night choir meetings at the church in order to prepare the music for Christmas day.

❧ **6** ❧

A Roadside Acquaintance

OF THE STOLEN HORSES we heard nothing. Word was sent to the city on the Saturday after the theft and the attack on Abel Strong, and John Spare paid to print in the City paper a notice which duly appeared under the words, "Stop Thief," with a small picture of a horse thief lashing his horse to a run, and pursued by a man firing a pistol. But that was the only pursuit ever made, for we had no clue to follow. My master also had the Germantown printer print some large notices, offering a reward for the horses, and these notices were distributed, and hung up in the taverns and stores of several counties, creating excitement in all our section of the country, but nothing more came of it.

I wondered sometimes whether I ought to speak to my master of having met Jim Ferrell on a Somerset road in England, but said nothing until one day he asked, as if the thought had only occurred to him;

"Richard, did you hear the dogs bark on the night the horses were stolen?" We had two young sheep dogs on the farm, neither of them more than two years old, both knowing and affectionate, with long memories, unforgiving dislikes, and several habits which were hard to break. If he could, one or the other would get upon my bed to sleep, and the odor of the dog would linger about the covers so that I could still smell him when I went to bed. Both were great barkers, and as they were made nervous by sudden noises, I afterward tried to break up their habit of barking furiously at nothing by shooting off a small charge of powder from a pistol. At the sound they would run to the house and seek shelter, not to reappear for an hour or more, and the remedy would sometimes be effective for several weeks. Why hadn't the dogs, which were in and out of the house every few minutes, no sooner being let in than they whined to be let out, given any warning the night of the horse stealing?

I asked my master how long he had the dogs and where he got them. He said he took them about six months before from a farmer in the back country, who had given up raising sheep. He added that he had heard the new hostler at the tavern to be from that part of the country. Then I asked quite innocently,

"And what might be the hostler's name?"

"I don't know what his last name is, I've heard Bane call him Jeremiah."

If he who had been Jim in England was now Jeremiah in America, there must be some sound reason for the change, and if he knew my master's dogs, or better still, if they knew him, it might be, in view of Jim's record in England, that we were near to suspecting why the dogs had given no warning to the house that something was out of the common way at the barn. So I began to fear that Jim Ferrell had not changed his heart with his name and thought it better to tell my master of my encounter with Jim in the English road, of the pulling up of the survey marks along my father's farm, and that I had never seen Jim again until I saw him standing in the tavern door with a candle lighting his face, while he answered William Barnes's questions.

When John Spare had considered this information he said:

"We will keep this just between ourselves until we know more of him. If he has plenty of rope, maybe he will hang himself."

After this, we of the choir worked faithfully at the Christmas music. David Wilkinson had gathered together above a dozen half-grown boys and girls from the farms, and was breaking them into the singing of several sacred choruses, and we thought everything was going well and were pleased with our own efforts.

Eunice Spare and I drove to the church in the sleigh, taking the two horses and covering the distance much more quickly than could be done in the summer. I never could tell beforehand how Eunice would look when she appeared suitably clad for our sleigh rides. She would leave the supper table, the Eunice Spare with whom I was by this time well-acquainted, and she would come down stairs in a different garb, a Eunice that I seemed to know hardly at all, of whom I felt a kind of awe, one to whom it was difficult to say the common words about common things, as I could do freely enough when she was making the butter or feeding her turkeys. This change came over her not only when we were going to the choir meeting or to church, but at other times, and might occur several times on the same day or from day to day. It always brought to me a feeling of strangeness and shyness, and if I had helped her into the sleigh and tucked the robes in well, I was relieved if the horses for a while took all my attention. After they had pulled on the reins for a half a mile, throwing balls of snow from their flying feet into the sleigh or over our heads, I would become more master of myself. By that time she would usually demand the reins, and they were no sooner in her hands than the horses, without a word from her, took a longer stride, in a way that was pretty to see under the December moon. Eunice was the best woman driver that I have ever seen except one, who, being stronger, could manage a dangerous horse, when the slighter frame of my master's daughter would have been unequal to the task. We drove back and forth many times to the church, and during the week before Christmas we younger people were busy on several evenings in placing about the church wreaths and strips of evergreen and holly. For the last, the men had to go a long way, as it did not grow in our vicinity. Theodore Morris was on hand while this adorning of the church was going on, handing the greens to Eunice Spare or asking her to hand them to him. But he never went with the men by day to gather any greens, and he never brought any to the church. Annie Bates spoke to me of this with a somewhat contemptuous look, and David Wilkinson gruffly said that he supposed Morris would get most of the credit for the work from the congregation. Eunice must have noticed what others saw, but she made no comment.

The musical part of the service was done without a flaw on Christmas day. I do not remember anything of the sermon. The truth is that between the minister and the choir there was no great cordiality. We thought that his part in the service only led up, or was an interruption, to our more brilliant performance, and I think the preacher had fathomed our feelings towards his share in the service, and sometimes what he said about the choir came back to us. However indifferent to the sermon, David Wilkinson and I and the two or three other men who intermittently sang with us may have been, or even the women, who were sometimes added to the choir, at least Eunice Spare and Annie Bates listened with every show of attention and respect.

After Christmas we settled down to the routine of our farm life, and the days were full enough to keep our minds and hands occupied, both the men and the women, we with our threshing and they with their spinning and quilting. John Spare or I took the wheat to the mill, and once a week, or once in two weeks, according to the weather, my master drove a waggon load of farm produce to the city market. Sometime in January, about three months after my arrival in America, he said that I should go to market with him the next time, learn the method of selling our produce, and drive home alone; while he would remain in the city for a few days to attend to some business and come home with some of the country people, who were sure to be returning to within easy walking distance of our farm. I was pleased to go both because of what I should see and learn and because I should have a chance to inquire about my chest, which by this time should have arrived, though my master's recent inquiries made of the Germantown printer had met with no favorable answer. On our way to the city we stopped at the printer's, but he had heard nothing of the chest. He advised me to go, after the market was over, to the ship's agent and inquire, which I did, but here again I was disappointed.

We had quickly sold our waggon load of produce at prices which were arrived at by consultation with other farmers.

Sometimes customers at my master's stall in the market would try to bargain with us, but they never offered to bargain over Eunice Spare's butter, being glad to get it because of its quality at the price asked, which was a better price than other good butter sold for. When the sales had been made, my master tied the money received in a bag, and placed it in my custody to be taken home, as he would soon have some payments to make, and he did not care to carry this bulk of small coins, which he would need for change at home, about the city with him.

I reminded him that the last time I had carried market money home, it was my father's money, and I had been attacked by Jim Ferrell, and only by good luck had escaped without a broken head and with a full purse. He thought there was little danger, and said:

"Richard, you will only travel by daylight, and in the daytime you will be safe. This afternoon you can only go as far as The Bell tavern before night sets in. You will find other farmers there, staying all night, and in the morning you will have company until you turn off on our by-road."

I told him that I would do the best I could, and we went our different ways, I to the ship's agent first, and then to the Bell. I was glad to reach the tavern, which I did a little after dark. We had left home at three o'clock that morning, and I had been riding or standing in the market ever since, and I was ready for a full supper and a sound sleep afterwards. The supper I got, but was disappointed about the sleep. The tavern was crowded with farmers, who, like myself, had been attending the city market. Every bed was taken, and every settee. Three of us were left without any place to sleep, unless we slept on the floor, and we could not do that until the more fortunate ones had disappeared for the night.

We three were drawn together by our ill luck, and we talked a little as to what we should do. One of the three, who had, like myself, drawn a blank in the lottery of beds, a mild spoken, honest-looking young man, whose English had a German sound, said that he had enough empty potato bags to make a fair bed on the floor. He told us that his name was John Cassell and that he lived some miles to the Eastward of my master's farm, in the German settlement. The second unlucky member of the trio, who was clad as a farmer, and carried a long whip with him, did not seem to be known by any of the dozen farmers at the inn, though he moved among them and talked with the men. He said that his name was Albert Judson, that he had not been to market, but was driving a single horse, which had gone lame, so that he had been compelled to leave it at a small farm two miles back towards the city, after which he had made his way on foot to The Bell, hoping to meet some acquaintance who would give him a lift on his way home.

After the farmers who had secured beds had gone to their rooms, we three made ready for the night by bringing in from the waggons all the potato bags we had to place between us and the hardness of the floor. There was a good fire in the fire-place and there were plenty of logs with which to replenish it. My companions were soon asleep, but though I was weary, my mind flew from one thing to another, from my master's money, no great sum, then to my missing chest, to my old home in England and back again to Eunice Spare, or to the choir meetings, or the strangeness of seeing Jim Ferrell so near my present home. Several times, as I almost fell asleep, a partly-burned log dropped between the andirons, and began to crackle and blaze anew in a way to drive off slumber. We had brought in the lap covers from the waggons for bed covering, and therefore I did not heed the draught along the floor from the room door to the chimney, but it was late when I lost consciousness. When I awoke the next morning the room was empty. Already the farmers had eaten their breakfasts and started homewards, among them the German Cassell, but when I went to get my breakfast my other roomate, Judson, was seated alone at one of the two long tables. We exchanged greetings, but when I had given some sufficient answer to his question how I had rested, he made no further attempt to continue the conversation. Perhaps, if he had done so, I with my master's money about me would have held aloof. Observing him by daylight, I began to take more notice of him than he took of me. His way of handling his knife and fork, and of eating his food and taking his tea, which he sipped out of a cup and not from the saucer, was different from the manners of most of our farmer folk. I do not mean that he was dainty as Eunice Spare was or her Aunt Mercy, but he did not set about the business of eating so directly as I myself did, and there were many men in our part of the country who did not try even as hard as I did, sometimes, not to show the hunger that grows in a man who lives out of doors. Sometimes he would stop eating altogether, and appear to be reflecting upon matters that had nothing to do with the food before him, which with us was not customary.

Partly to bring him back to the business in hand, and partly out of curiosity to hear what so thoughtful a man might have to say, I said to him, speaking in a somewhat loud tone, such as was needed to carry across the room:

"I find the food better than the lodging at the tavern."

It did not seem to me that he was going to respond to my advance, but presently as if from a height, almost like a person of quality, and not at all like a man who had slept on my potato bags in the same room with me, he gave some answer in a tone which indicated that he was indifferent whether I heard or not.

Now I have ever been willing to go as far as anyone to meet a man on equal terms, or to concede his merit if I knew him to be a superior person, but I have never been able to value as superiority that which I have seen nothing but the pretension of. Naturally I have a hearty voice, which has been strengthened by calling the cows, and by church singing. It was I that the miller came for the next spring to shout a message across the flood, when nobody else could be heard, to say that Adam Avery's boy was in the tree top on the island, and likely to be swept away, and to bring a boat, and saved the boy. I could have made the walls of the room at The Bell ring with my voice if I had been so minded, but with not more power than was required to hold his attention I said:

"Would you mind speaking a little more loudly?"

Remembering that the man had slept on my potato bags, it is possible that some of my feeling went into words. However that might be, he replied quite clearly;

"I said that the food would do well enough."

I could not quarrel with his words, although his manner of disdain may have merited a quarrel, and for want of something better to do I fell silent, but now and then noticed the man as I had opportunity. He had a long, rather narrow face, with a jaw that was a perfect oval from ear to chin, large eyes, that at one time were grey and at another green, and a prominent nose that was neither Roman nor pug. His voice was rich and full when he chose to use it, and I thought I should know him if I ever saw or heard him again.

He soon left the room, giving me a passing nod, as if he were hardly aware of my presence, so that I did not feel my importance increased. When I had finished my meal, I paid my reckoning, and when the horses were harnessed, resumed my homeward journey. A mile on the way, I overtook my bed fellow of the potato bags. I had a great mind to let him continue to walk for his impertinence, but it was the custom of the country to ask any foot goer to ride if there was a spare seat to offer, so I checked the horses and invited him to get in the waggon. Afterwards, I was amazed on thinking backwards over his gradual approach to something like cordiality, as if at first he was not sure that I was worthy of his confidence, then as if I were not so untrustworthy as I had at first appeared, then as if he need not be as close mouthed as he had been up to that time, and finally, as if I were a person to his liking, whom he would be pleased to meet again. I confess that as this gradual process and change were developed, it was flattering to me, and almost persuaded me that I possessed powers not before suspected.

Judson—I knew his name was Judson because he had told me so on the previous evening—said, after his heart had relented towards me a bit:

"No, I am not a farmer, but a factor. When I can find a farm that suits me I am going to be a farmer again. It's a safe pursuit, and profitable, too."

"Not as profitable as it ought to be for the work," I replied.

"Here my master and I were up at two o'clock yesterday morning. How many hours of labor did it take to grow and prepare for market what we took to the city? And how many pounds did we get for all this labor? Some, of course, but not many." I was not going to reveal the secrets of my master's business.

"Prices are better lately," he replied.

"Yes, but you carry twenty dozen eggs, and get only sixpence a dozen, now in the winter time. You sell fifty pounds of the very best butter that a skillful maid can make, and you get only a shilling a pound, which is more than the market price. Say you have thirty bushels of potatoes, what does that amount to at less than two shillings a bushel? Often they won't fetch that. Then you take a barrel of cabbage, which hardly counts at thrippence a head, and it may be a couple of hundred weight of pork—you know what you have to pay for hams and shoulders—as much as you can carry on a waggon, and two men drive twenty-five miles to the city, and one comes back with how much? Well, not enough to retire to the city with, and live on the interest."

I had no sooner said this than I knew that in the heat of argument I had said a foolish thing. Judson, however, appeared to be merely a philosophical person, who liked to discuss an abstract question, and I trusted that he had passed over my little sum in arithmetic without finding the answer, easy as it would have been to a surveyor.

By this time, it having taken over an hour for Judson's leniency towards my faults of outward manner to justify itself, we were nearly half way home. The wind had swung around to the South, bringing with it a warmth like that of Spring, and making a deep slush in the road. What with arguing and driving the horses at the same time, I became very warm in the heat of the sun, and taking off my outer great coat, and folding it, laid it in the waggon behind me. As I have said, I had been up early in the day, and had slept poorly on the night before. After a while, when we were going up Corson's long hill, Judson's voice seemed to have become a droning sound, like that of a bumble-bee on a warm June day. Then, I was awake again, and was conscious that I had missed the thread of the talk, as his voice now ran on in even tones upon some matter that had no bearing on what had been said before. Soon thereafter we came to a cross-road, where Judson said that he would alight, he having an acquaintance near by who would lend him a horse. He thanked me for his seat in the waggon, and we parted. As the sun was obscured by drifting clouds an hour later, I again put on my great coat, and felt in the deep pocket the heavy weight of the bag of coins, which I had wrapped in a colored handkerchief. I gave the bag to Eunice Spare to keep until her father's return. For safety, in case of thieves, she took it to her bedroom.

John Spare came back on Tuesday of the next week, just before supper time. After we had eaten he asked for the market money, and Eunice brought the bag in its wrapping from her room, and her father put it away safely in his strong box. On Thursday morning he opened it to make up a sum which he had to pay over on that day. On untying the bag he found that it was filled with leaded discs of different sizes, and when I saw them I knew I had been a fool, and got what satisfaction I could by moulding the metal into bullets.

❧ 7 ❧

The Shad Fishing

MY MASTER had to put off his settlement and tell the reason why, not being one to fail in meeting a money debt without good reason, and the story took flight. Whether it is so with other persons I know not. As to myself, through life I have remembered pleasant things, and forgotten the bitterness of disappointments, but the mortification of the loss of my master's money remained with me a long time, and even now, sometimes when I lie awake in the middle of the night, which I never did in my youth, the shame of it will come back, and I have to turn over and force my thoughts to something quieting.

Mercy Spare twitted me every now and then, unexpectedly, and mimicking the country pronunciation of the word "hold," played with my name by saying that I must learn to take a tighter *Holt* on my money, which, with the failure to hear anything of my missing chest, and my own money in the bottom of it, caused me to resolve to be more cautious. John Spare said that it might have happened to anybody, and his daughter, Eunice, looked disapprovingly at her aunt—so matters might have been worse.

At the church, Theodore Morris now paid some attention to me for the first time, asking questions about my adventure, stories of which in their journeys had departed from the actual happening. Was it true that I had been robbed by two gigantic men? And had I made a desperate resistance until overpowered by one seizing me from behind, while the other attacked me in front? And had I been left unconscious, and had I come to lying in the road, while the horses stood with the waggon nearly overturned, their noses against a bank? Had the robbers really got away with all that money?

"How much money?" I asked.

"Why, I am told that John Spare had sent home by you money he had drawn for the purchase of more land, that you had the market money besides, and that the robbers got enough to set up a business within the city."

I had never been used to dealing with mental indirection, but the coming to America, the loss of my chest and the excitement of the robberies had started a new alertness in my mind, and I suspected that Theodore Morris had heard none of these things that he pretended to be so curious about. It was Eunice Spare who came to my relief by saying:

"Now, Theodore, all that is nonsense. I think people are silly to tell such tales. The thief got no such sum of money, Richard Holt had been up early and late, and fell asleep for a few minutes. The money was in the pocket of his great coat. The thief just stole it and put off."

"Oh, that was the way it happened. Not so bad as it seemed. A clever fellow, that robber, whoever he was! Shouldn't wonder if it was one of the Doanes!" and he laughed aloud. "He asked for a ride, and you invited him to get into the waggon, and he stole your money, and you knew nothing about it!"

He laughed again very heartily, but I did not feel any stirrings towards mirthfulness in myself, and the singing that morning so lacked the usual spirit that David Wilkinson's face bore a look of discontent. During sermon time I began to wonder if the robber had been one of the Doanes, as Theodore Morris had suggested. I had heard that several of the notorious family were artful in assuming to be what they were not, and could play a part to serve a purpose with a skill that could deceive the most knowing. I began to see that the indifference of Doane, or whoever he was, to my presence at The Bell might have been a pretence, and that his walking off ahead, on a road where I should presently overtake him and invite him to ride, with no trouble to him except a little wholesome, physical exercise, was the best plan he could adopt to avoid arousing any doubt or distrust of him.

I had been told that the Doanes often disguised themselves by wearing different colored wigs on different occasions, and by selecting for wear from their plunder garments suitable to the part they had decided to play for the time. Sometimes when working the road alone, a Doane was said to appear where he was least expected as a Quaker preacher; at another time he was an honest farmer, or a cattle dealer, or a Virginian travelling Northward on business of the colony, or a gentleman on a visit to a family in distress.

Several persons in the three counties had encountered the same Doane, Moses, or one of his numerous brothers, twice within two days, and had not known he was the same man. I thought that I might be deceived by a disguise of the person, but I had a good memory for voices, and could remember a voice, heard only once before, after a long interval when I would be very uncertain about the face. So I felt confident of remembering the voice of the robber, and thought, if it ever should become known that he was really one of the Doanes, that my humiliation would be lessened, for it was rather a mark of honor, and reflected credit on a man to be robbed by a Doane. The robbers, whoever they were, acted as if they intended merely to prevent us from falling into too dull a state of existence, and therefore did not honor us so often as to give us time to become used to them.

The rest of the winter wore away peacefully. George Heacock, Samuel Pearson, and Walter Jenkins missed their stolen hunting horses, for they could not join the fox hunters in the Great Valley that winter, and remained in a depressed state of mind, manifested when I met them by a gloomy level of talk. Spring came on all at once after a warm rain, which let the ice out of the creek and branch, with the mighty roar of a great flood, at the time Adam Avery's boy was rescued from the tree top on the island by the aid of my voice. Presently the waters cleared, and the shad began running up the river for as much as thirty miles above the mouth, and how much further I cannot say.

One day in May, Mercy Spare said to her brother:

"John, the Dogwood is in full blossom."

"What then, Sister Mercy?", he asked.

"When the Dogwood is in blossom the shad fishing season is at its height. Can we go to the fishing shore on Saturday?"

We made ready on the day before, the women preparing a basket-full of food, which we were to supplement at the shore with a shad freshly taken from the water. The two boys went along, and we had a carriage load. The fishing shore was ten miles away. We crossed the river at the ford, and then going down the right bank of the stream for the distance of a mile and a half, came to the place where the people living thereabouts were accustomed to put out a seine from the shore, and take the shad as they ascended the river to spawn. Herring, too, were taken, coming a little earlier than the shad, but they were not much esteemed, and by some were spread upon the ground to enrich the soil. I have seen large herring far inland, in a small brook that a man could leap across. A large concourse of people had gathered at the shore before we arrived, some to buy a fish or two fishes for the table when the seine had been hauled in, and many merely to have the pleasure of seeing what was going on without its costing anything. In this part of the river there was a long island, which made a deep current between it and the main shore, and the shad ascended this channel in great numbers. When we had tied the horses in a safe place, we joined the throng of people already at the water's edge. Theodore Morris, whose home was not far off, came to show Eunice Spare what was to be seen, though there was nothing but what was in plain sight of everybody. He asked me if I had heard of my robbers yet, and without waiting for an answer, turned to my master, and told him that the landlord of the Red Lion was there, and had offered four shillings for the heaviest shad taken that morning. No shad was worth any such price, so the offer served as a fillip to curiosity, and everybody experienced an agreeable sense of something coming to pass.

The rowers took the seine through the water several times, and caught many shad. Each time the seine was drawn in, the landlord of The Red Lion exclaimed loudly,

"Remember men! Four shillings for the first choice!" and everybody stood on tip toe, trying to see over the fishermens' shoulders what might be the size and quality of the catch.

Presently Mercy Spare exclaimed:

"I can see nothing for the people. Let us go back to yonder little knoll where we can look over their heads."

We walked back to the slight elevation—the Spares, Theodore Morris and I—and watched while the seine was taken through the waters again and again.

"John," said his sister, "there's that deaf and dumb man with the fishermen again. He was here last year. They call him "The Dummy," though he's as handy with an oar as the best of them."

She pointed out the man to me. He wore large, colored spectacles, as if to keep the bright sunlight, reflected from the water, from his eyes.

When he turned away from us to go to the boat, I fancied I saw something familiar in the shape of his back, but took no further interest in him. Mercy Spare, however, was curious and approaching one of the fishermen, she asked who the man was that wore the spectacles.

"That fellow" came the reply, "he's a queer one" and tapping his forehead, he added, "he's not all there. He can't hear a sound, or speak a word. He came this morning, and made signs to let us know that he wanted to take an oar for a share of the fish. He's right spry at an oar. Nobody knows his name, or where he's from. We call him 'The Dummy.' "

Drawing nearer, I heard the spectacled fisherman occasionally making the unpleasant throat sounds of the stone deaf, and convinced that I had been mistaken in fancying that I had seen a resemblance to some one known to me, I returned to the family group. At noon the hauling of the seine ceased for the day. All the fishes taken were divided by count and apparent size into as many piles as there were fishermen. This being done, one of the men turned his back upon the fish, and another called out, "Whose pile is this?" and the other having declared whose it should be, the next pile was awarded to another of the fishermen, and so on, until each man had his allotment of fish in a way to ensure fairness, and leave no hard feelings. All the piles had been distributed except one, and now the question was asked, "Whose is this?" The awarder called out, "That's 'The Dummy's.' I declare I nearly forgot The Dummy,' " and taking the deaf mute by the arm, he led him to the pile of fish, and by pointing first to the fish, and then poking the mute in the breast, made him clearly understand that he was the owner of the last pile awarded. Each fisherman then searched for his largest fish, and when it had been found carried it to be weighed upon the landlord's steel-yard. The last to come forward to put in his claim for the landlord's reward was the deaf mute. The fish he carried did not appear to be quite as large as some that had been weighed previously, but the steel-yard showed that it was several ounces heavier than the heaviest of these. Landlord Lane called out the weight so that all could hear, and announcing that "The Dummy" had won the prize, handed him four silver shillings. The crowd laughed good humouredly, and several persons shouted, "Good for the Dummy!" The mute behaved rather foolishly as he pocketed his reward, making inarticulate sounds from his throat, and dancing about in a silly fashion, until attention was turned from him by the departure of most of the throng for their homes.

When the people had dispersed, except the fishermen and a few others, among whom were the landlord of The Red Lion, a good liver and host, named Lane, the Spare family and myself and Theodore Morris, the landlord invited us to help him eat the prize shad, saying he would build a fire, and soon have the fish ready. We gathered a pile of fagots and larger wood, which had been cast up along the river shore, and set the fire to burning, while the landlord undertook to open and clean the shad. Mercy and Eunice Spare stood by, and watched to see that he did this properly. He had hardly cut into the fish before we heard from him exclamations of surprise and an oath or two, and immediately thereafter the merriest peals of laughter from the women. John Spare, Theodore Morris and I hastened to join them, and we, too, were amazed to see the landlord engaged in emptying out of the partly opened fish, not what would be natural to look for, but some ounces of bright, clean pellets of lead in the shape of bird shot. My master laughed heartily when it was clear to him, as it was to all of us, that the mute had poured the shot in to the shad's mouth to make sure of the landlord's reward.

The landlord sought him wrathfully, but the other fishermen said that "The Dummy" had gone, taking with him only a couple of fish from the pile that had been awarded to him, and leaving the rest for any one who might choose to possess them. The landlord was altogether put out by the discovery of the lead in the fish's belly, thinking there had been an abuse of his generosity and public spirit. Therefore, he did not join in our laughter, but declared that he would have his four shillings back, which he never did. Although his temper had been tried, he went on after a bit with preparing the fish under the eyes of the women, accepting their corrections in a proper spirit. Then he made the shad fast to a flat piece of Hickory wood, long enough and wide enough to hold the outspread shad, and yet leave some margin of board beyond. When this was properly done, he stood the board nearly upright before the fire. The shad began to give forth an appetizing smell, and Mercy and Eunice Spare hastened to spread on the ground the cloth, the pewter plates, the bread and potatoes, which by this time were well roasted. In spite of its many bones, I thought that for substance and flavor I had never eaten a fish equal to the shad; and there is a way to manage the bones, too, as I learned by practice. But to be at its best, the shad must be eaten close to its home waters, and be cooked on a board in the way that I have described, being careful not to scorch it.

Landlord Lane completely recovered his good humour, owing to the excellence of the cooking, and he told several proper tales with liveliness and wit, after which we men helped to wash the pewter and make all tidy, burning up the litter before we started homewards.

I do not know how it happened, but when we were two thirds of the way across the river we missed the ford. The off horse lost his footing and the carryall slanted until the water ran in, and Mercy Spare was frightened and cried out, though Eunice made no sign. I managed to get the horses where they could stand, but was in doubt about trying the waters ahead. I had just handed the lines to John Spare, intending to sound the stream on foot, while he should drive after me, where it was safe, when a horseman, who had been following us unheard, rode by the carriage to the horses' heads, led them directly up the stream some fifty feet, and then safely to the shore. We saw at once that our guide was the deaf mute, whose shot laden fish had won the landlord's four shilling reward.

"It is most fortunate," said Mercy Spare, "that he overtook us. We should all have been drowned. John!" she called. "How are we to thank him? He can't hear a word. Look at him, John! Who would take him for a poor fisherman! See how well he sits his horse! What a handsome figure he has, and how graceful—like a gentleman! John, you must give him a shilling." Secure in the deaf mute's inability to hear a word, her tongue ran on in high pitched comment upon our guide's appearance, manner and service to us until we reached the shore, when she said, "Now, John! Have your shilling ready!"

Our horses had stopped of their own accord to breathe after the stiff pull through the river sand and deep water, when our guide turned about, took off his hat, and making a bow to us as he declined the proferred shilling said in a voice, which I at once knew to be that of my companion at The Bell tavern, who had called himself Judson, and who on the way home, had relieved me of my master's money; "Holt, once you gave me a lift on the road. I have now had a chance to return the favour. That time, maybe, I put you to some inconvenience.

If so, it was all in the way of business, and I hope you bear me no ill will."

Wheeling his horse about, he rode rapidly away. Eunice seemed to look upon the adventure as a cause for mirth. Her eyes sparkled as she watched her aunt, who for a time was as dumb as our guide had been at the fishing shore. Eunice broke the silence by saying to her aunt, slyly:

"You were right, Aunt Mercy. He's quite the gentleman, with a fine figure, a good seat in the saddle and perfect manners."

Her aunt was in no mood for jesting. "Eunice Spare, never mention this to me again," she said sternly. "John, do you think he heard me?"

"Of course he did," her brother replied. "He heard nothing but good of himself, and no harm is done."

❧ 8 ❧

The Flutter of Drums

THERE FOLLOWED a season of steady work, and nothing more of the Doanes, except that in the lower end of the next county, but not so far away that we did not hear of it, three weeks after it happened, a house had been robbed and one of the defenders shot. But this, occurring at a remote place, was not our concern. Neither had I heard of my chest. The Germantown printer told me that if word came of it he would send me a message, so I had given up asking about it, fearing to weary him; and now I had almost given up thought of getting my property again, and had in a manner become reconciled to the loss; and after I had been relieved of John Spare's money I was less inclined than before to say anything of the money of my own that had been lost with the chest.

The wheat was ripe and fit to cut the first week in July. We began to cut on the fourth of that month. My master had fifteen reapers to help him, and the women had help in preparing the prodigious quantity of food necessary for such a number of men. My master stood at the head of the table and said a grace, before all sat down, and he carved the meat for all, when, no doubt, he would have liked better to take his own dinner restfully after a long morning in the wheat field. We began work as soon as might be after daylight, and we stopped when we could see to work no longer, and every reaper was proud of what he could do, and would have been ashamed to fall behind the rest. The women did not eat with us during harvest, when the men came in sweaty from their hot work, after washing at the well, and combing out their wet locks. It had not been so hot during the hay harvest in June as it was in the wheat harvest afterwards, but the pace set by Jared Bush, who led the mowers across the field, was one to make a man wonder if he could hold out until he reached the end of the swath. This first summer in America went hard with me, and what with the work, and an eagerness of all to press forward, and a fiercer sun than we knew in England, I lost flesh, and longed for bed and rest to such a degree, that I had to give up the choir singing, and while I saw Eunice Spare every day, it would come over me, as I fell asleep almost as soon as supper was over, that I had scarcely seen her at all. It was then I think that I began to carry about with me a mental picture of her. But my appetite did not fail me, and I believed that I should come round again, and wished for frost.

After the wheat, came the oats. Then the potatoes were to be taken up, the fall ploughing was to be done, and the buckwheat gathered in; and somehow, by keeping at it all, the work was accomplished, with me a better man than I had been in the spring, and my master well satisfied, and we were making all snug for another winter, with the barn full and over running, and I had time to try my voice with Do, Re, Mi, Fa, Sol, La, Ti, Do again.

Abroad, that is with many people who were not farmers and therefore had time to think of our welfare and how our condition might be improved, matters too vast for us rightly to understand were under way by this time, and slowly we learned by much teaching that we were being oppressed. It must have been so, for presently there was much talk of raising an army in the Colonies to resist the oppression by England that had been discovered, and one of our own wardens was going to be a Colonel. When our neighbors consulted John Spare, and asked him to point out the true inwardness of the situation, he recommended that each man attend to his own business as strictly as he could, since there were already a sufficient number of persons who were attending to the business of other people.

The men who had anything at stake were disposed to listen to this, and declared it to be sound advice; but there were enough of the other kind to keep the ball rolling to the edge, and over. Judge Morris held much the same view that John Spare held at that time, though afterwards they drew apart.

More and more, men drifted to one side or the other, and after they had taken their position, began to search for reasons to justify themselves, and in their talk to condemn their opponents, which led to the breaking of friendships and the deepening of animosities. And presently there was an English army marching, now on one side of the river, then on the other, and an American army on the side opposite, and the Doanes making the best of this state of things. The city market was cut off from us, and John Spare found money hard to come by.

By this time my labor had repaid John Spare for my passage money, and he was no longer my master, or I his servant; and I found that my surveying instruments came of use at last, when I was employed to lay out a new cross road and survey a farm or two. But new enterprises fell off; farm land was not in so much demand as it had been, owing to the decrease of the inflow of emigrants, and the general checking of affairs. Therefore, I continued to work for John Spare, he paying me wages now, but in the new money and having to draw on his savings, he told me, because of the interruption to trade. The English army paid for flour with coin, and we should have liked to have some of this, but the trade with the English was attended by difficulties, besides running counter to American sentiment. Not that we were in any want of food or fire or clothing. All these we had from the farm, though we had to go without tea, which was a deprivation to Mercy Spare, and she let it be known.

Being my own man now, I felt more at my ease in the presence of her niece, Eunice, and was not so overcome as I had been with backwardness when I drove her or, as often happened, she drove the horses to the church for choir practice. Some of our men singers had already gone off to the war, but David Wilkinson was too old to go, and did the best he could with the singers who were left behind. Neither had Theodore Morris gone to fight; and Eunice Spare, who was the staunchest American in our household, would sometimes rally him about it, and he would fail to appear at the church for several Sundays in succession.

After one of these absences she said to him upon his reappearance: "Why Theodore, I thought you had gone to the war."

"Not yet, Eunice. Would you like me to go?" and he asked this question in a tone of tenderness, which I had never heard in his voice, which was usually a mocking voice.

"I am sure, Theodore, that an officer's uniform would be becoming to you."

"Which color would be more becoming to me, do you think? Scarlet or Blue and Buff?"

"When you have put on the uniform and wear it here to church, maybe I shall tell you" she answered.

Now, if Theodore Morris put on a scarlet uniform it was certain that he would not appear in it at our church, unless the troops of England marched with him, and in that case Eunice Spare would not be present to pronounce judgment upon the fit of his clothes, and he had his answer.

Before me, Eunice Spare was ever considerate in what she said about the English. She and her father both took it for granted that, having come but lately from England, and now being an American, likely to spend my life in this country, all that could be expected of me was that I should hold the position of a neutral spectator, awaiting whatever fortune might be in store for the colonies. Eunice never talked to me about putting on a uniform, as she had talked to Theodore Morris. On the contrary, she had once gone out of her way to express her understanding of my situation, torn between affection for the home of my family, and my own home until a few months before, on the one side, and the merging of my interests in my new home, on the other. I thanked her, telling her that I was indeed in the deep waters of doubt, and some distress of mind, but perhaps, time would make the way clear. Whereupon, she held out her hand to me in the warmth of womanly sympathy, and listened while I told her of my English home, of my dead father and mother, and their goodness, and of my brother Robert, whom I had not heard from since the war broke out.

Should I live to be as old as John Spare is now, and that is well above eighty years, I shall never forget that mild, moonlit evening in the autumn, already far in the past, when she and I sat on the little porch of her father's home, and my troubles brought her closer to me than she had ever been before. We could hear in our silence the purr of the low water, falling over the mill-dam, a good distance off. Sometimes, the soft breeze brought the sound to us, and sometimes, carried it away from us. As we talked, we would forget it, and as we grew silent, it came clearly to us again. If he can find a maid to listen to him, or a maid's brother, or father, for that matter, a man will talk long, and when I grew ashamed of my volubility, Eunice asked me a question, or made some comment, showing her sympathy, and I started off again in a scandalous flow of words, only being recalled to an humbler state when John Spare came to the door and said that it was growing late, and time for all honest folk to be in bed.

For all my distress of mind and conflict of doubts, I went to sleep with a lighter heart than I had felt since the war began.

❧ 9 ❧

The Judge's Guest

WHILE OTHER PEOPLE were taking up arms, or fleeing to Nova Scotia, and the two hostile armies were marching up and down the country, as if they sought a battle or sought to avoid one, a man could hardly tell which, the Doanes, as I have said, had grown bolder and more enterprising than ever, preying upon the Revolutionists usually, but not averse to relieving a fat Tory of a well–filled purse.

In September of the year 1777, Judge Morris was kept at home with an attack of gout. On a Wednesday afternoon he saw from his window a small cavalcade of uniformed horsemen ride up his driveway, and knew that they were British officers. One of them he took for an officer of rank. Confined to his chair, with his bandaged foot resting on a stool, he called:

"Pompey! Pompey! Damn the boy! Where is he? Pompey! Open the door for the officers!"

Pompey soon returned with General Howe's compliments to Judge Morris. The General followed close upon Pompey's heels, several officers coming close behind him, and said:

"No apology needed, Judge! Painful complaint, but seldom fatal! Recommend a change from Madeira! Major Montressor, Judge Morris! Colonel Plunket! Judge! Lord Pelham, Judge! The damned Rebels, Judge, may keep us here for a few days. Am looking for a headquarters house. All the houses around here are too small—nothing but stone cabins."

So it came to pass that General Howe made his headquarters at Judge Morris's house, and the excitement and honor of it all cured the Judge's gout, and the next day he was hobbling about with the aid of a staff. The spaciousness of the rooms, the table, and the Judge's wines were to General Howe's taste, and when his army marched on a few days later, the soldier expressed his appreciation of his host's hospitality by saying that he hoped he might have as good luck next time, but hardly expected it.

With Lord Pelham, Judge Morris came to a good understanding by Thursday, which, considering that he had never seen General Howe's subordinate until Wednesday afternoon, shows that they were two men of the same lofty ideas, though Lord Pelham was only about thirty-five years of age and the Judge long past his meridian. General Howe would call to his aid: "See here, Pelham! How's this, Pelham! Damn me, Pelham, isn't that order ready yet?"

Judge Morris on the other hand would say: "My Lord, try this '57 Madeira!" or "Do you think, my Lord, that the General will take Philadelphia?" and Lord Pelham would answer:

"Sure of it—take it any time he wants it."

Lord Pelham had a long narrow face, an oval jaw and large reflective eyes, that were grey or a greyish green, and a prominent nose.

When the army had marched, starting General Washington on a false scent up the river, and had slipped into Philadelphia, Judge Morris could not recall ever having seen a young man as agreeable as Lord Pelham, and said as much to his son, Theodore.

The Judge was less pleased afterwards, when he learned that the American army was in the vicinity, four miles away, encamped for the winter. He had changed his wine, and his gout had not come back, so he could go about on his horse. On a Saturday in February he had just ridden out of his lane and had barely entered the main road, over which he was riding slowly because it was frozen and rough, when he saw approaching him with equal slowness, a horseman in citizen's dress, and that was becoming a somewhat uncommon sight.

"That cannot be Lord Pelham," said the Judge, aloud in his surprise. "No! Why it is!" and he hurried forward as fast as he dared ride.

"My Lord, why run this risk? The American troops are on yonder hills. Their pickets are out in every direction. You may be recognized. Out of uniform too, and in the American lines!"

The Judge's concern, expressed by his words, was also conveyed by his agitated tones. The sombre face of the other horseman lighted with a smile.

"You think it dangerous?" he asked.

"It is, my Lord. Any minute a body of Americans may come down this road. Come back with me. Stay until opportunity offers to go on in safety. Believe me, your peril is great. A man may be hanged as a spy under such conditions."

The other shrugged his shoulders at this, and the Judge turning his horse, the two rode quickly to the Judge's house, where his guest entered without being seen by the farm-hands.

"You have lost flesh a little, since you were here, my Lord!"

"I really believe I have. There has been much hard riding to do."

"Yes, a little flesh, and I could almost have said a half inch in height," and the Judge laughed. "It's the other way with some of the Americans, I know. The little men have become bigger. They think so anyway" and the Judge's laugh was louder. "Wayne, Mifflin, Cadwalader—I've known them all since they were boys, and never thought to see them set the world on fire, except Wayne, maybe."

"It's not hard to start a fire," said the guest. "It's harder to put it out."

"My son, Theodore, has gone to help put it out since you were here. Have you happened to meet him in the city?"

"No, but Montressor told me that he was with the army, and doing well. Do you look for him to come home soon?"

"Not while the Americans are so near. He could ride up the other side of the river, cross above, and come down, but it would be dangerous. No, he won't come now."

Catching sight of his own face in the mantel glass opposite, there quickly faded from the guest's features an expression which was not that of regret.

"A promising young man, Judge; he is sure to rise."

"Thank you, my Lord. It pleases me that he is seen with favor by one so near the General. I hope that his conduct may be creditable. May I tell you something, in confidence, that has disturbed me. I have few friends left here now with whom I can talk about it. Sometimes, you know, it does an old man good to be garrulous."

The guest murmured a sympathetic reply, and the old man went on:

"Theodore could do well, and I hope, now that he is with the English army and has something to occupy his attention, that he will forget his fancy for a young woman, one Eunice Spare, whose home is near the church which we attend. She is a maiden of merit, comely in appearance, and above her station in life, which is that of a daughter of a plain farmer. Not but what her father is a man of merit, true and reliable. He is all that. There is no better man so far as manhood goes. But there is a matter connected with Eunice Spare which I cannot divulge—no stain upon her, mind you—something, which only two persons living know—John Spare and I—and we are bound to secrecy for a time—something which makes it unseemly my son should marry her. I am telling you this to ask your assistance. Theodore will be guided by the advice of one in your high position, who is older than himself. I cannot tell him all the reasons for discountenancing his attentions to the young woman, I have shown my dissatisfaction. Perhaps, too much. He thinks that I look for him to seek a wife in his own circle, and he is willful."

Judge Morris was not a man who often asked for help. He was now broken by the war. He felt the separation from the friends of a lifetime, who had given him up as one of the staunchest of England's supporters among Americans. His wife was long dead, and his son was gone. He was lonely, and troubled by a situation in which he did not know what was best to do. It is doubtful if he would have spoken at all had he taken time to think twice. He had not thought, but had yielded to a sudden impulse to unbosom himself in the presence of a sympathetic listener, with whose cause he was in almost complete accord, and for whom, personally, as a man of exalted station at home, who had given up comfort and luxury to lie upon a soldier's bed, and perhaps meet a soldier's death, he had respect and admiration.

The recipient of this sudden confidence conducted himself in a manner worthy of it, and after a little natural hesitation, assured the father that he would do what he could, and then in a gayer voice, made light of young men's passing fancies, and said that the youth in the stirring times ahead of him would soon forget the maiden.

"I thank you, my Lord. I am doubly glad that we met, on your account and on my son's."

At an early hour that night, the Judge's visitor pleaded fatigue, and was shown to his room. The Judge poked the fire and sat before it until it burned low, when he, too, made his way up the stairs. His heavy tread was heard awhile, and then the household grew quiet. The old moon rose about two o'clock the next morning. An hour later it was shining in the front windows of the bedrooms of the Morris house. Some of the rooms were unoccupied, the chamber doors standing wide open and letting the moonlight into the hall-way. In the wainscot, a mouse nibbled at the wood in the shadow, but the moon would soon uncover the spot where he was at work. The mouse at work, and the Judge at rest, breathing heavily in the slumber of a stout old man, made the only sounds. No other sound was made when a chamber door opened, and the Judge's guest appeared fully clad, or when, after listening at the Judge's door he opened it and entered the room. The Judge's watch and seals were hanging where their owner always hung them at night. A wallet and bunch of keys lay on the table. The Judge's guest went quietly out of the room, closing the door behind him. Though he moved as quietly along the hall, the mouse heard him, and became even more quiet than the man now finding his way down the stairs. They were stout stairs of oak, and gave no warning of descending foot-steps. In the room below, the man lit the candle which he carried, and choosing a key from the bunch that had lain on the table in the Judge's bed room, he opened the Judge's secretary. Here were some coins and a roll of paper money and the Judge's silver snuff box. Having no further use for the keys, the man laid them upon the secretary, and helping himself to a sheet of paper, a quill and ink, he sat down and wrote a letter. Saying aloud that it was an execrable pen, he mended it with the Judge's pen knife, and resumed his writing. Apparently, it was an amusing and an important letter. For he wrote it with deliberation, and once or twice, looking upwards for a thought, laughed silently. When he had done, he folded the letter, sealed it with the Judge's seal, addressed it in a fair hand to "The Honourable Samuel Morris—To be called For," and left it on the secretary. Carrying his candle to the hall door, he carefully drew the bolt, letting the moonlight into the hall. He did not need the candle any longer, so he took it back to the secretary, set it down, and thoughtfully blowing it out, left the house through the only doorway by which a guest should make his exit, and closed the front door of his host's house quietly behind him.

Upstairs, the Judge slept until his usual hour for arising—even a little beyond that hour. He looked to see the time of day.

"Bless me," said the Judge "did I leave my watch down stairs again last night!" He could not remember. His wallet was not on the bedroom table, nor his bunch of keys. "Well! Well!," said the Judge, "I must be failing." When he was dressed, he bustled into the hall-way, and seeing that his guest's door was still closed, he listened, but hearing no sound, knocked three times. There was no response. "My Lord," he called, "It's a fine morning, my Lord."

Receiving no reply, he thought that Lord Pelham must have gone below, and knocking again, he opened the door to find the room empty. Blaming himself for inhospitality for sleeping so late, he hurried down the stairs, expecting to find Lord Pelham in the room below. That room was also empty. Then the Judge's eye fell upon the open secretary, a sight which he did not understand at all. He might forget other things at his time of life, his watch and his keys, but he had never forgotten to lock his secretary. Then the Judge picked up the letter addressed, "The Honourable Samuel Morris—To be Called For." "To be Called For," he repeated aloud. "What can that mean?" He opened and read the following letter.

Morris Hall
February 14th, 1778

Dear Sir:

It has been Necessary that I should make an early start and get on my way, and have thought it better not to Disturb you. I trust you will overlook my hasty Departure without bidding you Farewell, but these are trying times, and a man cannot always stand upon the Order of his going. I take this means to thank you for your kind Hospitality.

If I see your son, Theodore, I will bear in mind the Purport of your conversation about his affairs.

With much Respect, I am
your Humble and Obedient Servant,
Moses Doane

To the Honourable
Samuel Morris.

❧ 10 ❧

"Mr. Morris and Mr. Holt"

ALL THE INS AND OUTS of the night's lodging which Judge Morris gave to Moses Doane, how it came about, and what was said, the one to the other, we did not learn at once, but afterwards, when the two sides of the story had been put together. Some news of the adventure spread quickly, especially when the Judge sent to the taverns and stores of the country a printed description of Doane's appearance, with the offer of a reward to anybody who would take him. John Spare brought home from the blacksmith's shop one of these sheets, and I read:

"Age about 25. Slender build. Narrow face. Prominent nose. Jaw oval. Smooth tongue. Can assume manners of them above him. Goes by different names. When last seen rode a Roan horse. Liberal reward to any that will apprehend said Moses Doane and cause his detention."

I have never read a description of men, or of a landscape, or of an occurrence, which much resembled what I have seen of the object described, and I have blamed myself for my own lack. So now I read the large print slowly and carefully that I might take it all in, and know the man, if it happen I should meet him in the road. Suddenly there came over me a great thought, and I flattered myself that my powers of perception might yet be of service to me. The man, Judson, who had slept on my potato bags at The Bell tavern, who rode with me behind John Spare's horses, had parted from me, taking John Spare's money, and who had played so well the part of a deaf mute at the fishing shore, if I could but put my hands on him, might be the means of winning for me the reward offered by Judge Morris. The Judge's description of Moses Doane corresponded in every particular with my recollection of the man who had told me that his name was Judson. Judson was "The Dummy," who had guided us at the river ford, as I had known from his voice. Now if Moses Doane had the same voice, then I could be certain. Any room for doubt was soon to be removed.

It soon turned out that Judge Morris had been mistaken about his son's going into the English army. The proof of this was that Theodore appeared at church on the very next Sunday, and a number of Sundays afterwards, and was more attentive to Eunice Spare than ever. Long after the war was over we knew, but we did not know it then, that he had gone to the city and had spoken to the officers, among them the real Lord Pelham who, in physical appearance might have been twin to Moses Doane, and they had advised against his plan of going into the field.

Major Montressor, the engineer officer, said to him:

"No, Morris, it won't do. In a year or two the Rebels will submit. If you fight against them they will never forgive you. You will have to go to Nova Scotia or to England. If you do not fight them, your father and you can do much to reconcile the colonies to their fate."

Colonel Plunkett and Lord Pelham agreed with the engineer officer, and instead of becoming a soldier, Theodore Morris went home again without anybody but his father knowing of the object of his journey. It was startling news that his father had to tell him. That Pelham had a double in the colonies, it afterwards appeared, was already known to some of the British officers, and Lord Pelham himself had heard of his remarkable resemblance to Doane from fellow officers, who earlier had held a meeting with the man, thinking he might be of some service to the British cause, but this expectation had been abandoned with the growth of the highwayman's ill repute. The Judge's mortification would have kept him quiet; his duty to the people required that he should endeavor to capture the thief, and the

Judge set duty above inclination. So the public notices were scattered broad-cast.

Doane's depredations theretofore had been committed against humble people. Now that he had broken out of his proper sphere of work, the courts, the sheriff and the constables might begin in earnest to keep a look-out for him, something which Doane, for all his wit, had overlooked. Very likely, without taking forethought, he had yielded to sudden temptation and opportunity, and the enjoyment of the affair.

After helping Eunice Spare out of the carriage at the church door on Sunday morning, I drove on to the sheds, and tied and blanketed the horses. On coming back, I saw all the members of the church choir, David Wilkinson, Eunice Spare, Annie Bates and the others, standing at the door in an excited group, listening to Theodore Morris, who was telling about the robbery of his father's house. My time as a Redemptioner now being a thing of the past, and almost forgotten by some because it was so common, between Theodore Morris and me it had been for quite a while "Mr. Morris" and "Mr. Holt," all very polite.

Eunice called to me as I approached:

"Richard Holt! Hurry! Come, hear this dreadful story!"

This was before we had seen the reward notice, which John Spare did not bring home until the next week, for it was necessary that a man ride to the city, have it printed, wait until the printer could finish the work, and then bring the bundles home in his saddle-bags. Quickening my pace at Eunice's call, I came up to the group, and asked:

"What has happened, Mr. Morris?"

His aspect of reserve seemed to increase with each step of my approach, as if he were burdened with weighty matters, which he had rather not unfold to me. Nevertheless he retold the tale of the robber, not as I have written it down from subsequent hearings, but the substance of it, and that briefly, as if he were not proud to tell it. Remembering how he had speared me with questions when I, myself, had fallen into the hands of a thief, I asked him some of the questions which he had asked me, over again, as I could readily do from often thinking of them.

"How many robbers did you say there were, Mr. Morris?"

"Only one, Mr. Holt, unless he had an accomplice, and from what father says I think that is doubtful."

"And there were servants in the house, men and women, and men at the barn, and nobody saw him come or go, and he escaped scatheless, with his booty to join the headless horse–man, the mischievous ghost of Warner's Mill, that lets the water out of the race at night, and all the rest of the spirits of the air! Was the booty large, Mr. Morris?"

"Of no great value, Mr. Holt. Our country is on the downward road when a man's house is not safe. The Rebels have brought it about. Things are better done in England."

Now I had not always found an English road entirely free of foot-pads, but I did not care to refute Mr. Morris with my own experience, and let it pass. Nor did I feel called upon to defend the Rebels, as he called the Americans who were in arms against England. But because of his remembered mirth over my own adventure and my loss of John Spare's money, I said:

"I have always heard, Mr. Morris, that the Doanes were thorough Tories, and only preyed on the Rebels."

Here Eunice Spare spoke up with some show of indignation:

"I won't have you, Richard Holt, or you, Theodore, calling our people Rebels. I shan't listen to it. Come, Annie! Let us go inside."

By this time the people were coming to church. Theodore Morris had to tell his story again and again, and the hearers did not seem to tire of it's repetition, as I did. David Wilkinson hung upon his words, and we missed the choir practice, and it looked from the number of persons who stood about with mouths agape, that unless Theodore Morris could be persuaded to leave off, the preacher would not have many hearers. It was now time for the service to begin, and we choir singers had to draw away, to David Wilkinson's disappointment.

When Eunice Spare and I were driving homewards, I asked

her if Theodore Morris had come into the church. She said that she did not know, and I was pleased over a slight thing, for I thought that many a duller maiden than Eunice Spare would have known whether her lover was in the church. From my position in the choir loft, the Morris family pew was plainly visible, and I saw that he was not seated in it. Eunice, standing further to the front, could see nearly the whole congregation, and if Theodore had come in late, and taken a back pew, the eye of love would not have missed him. At least, so I thought, until I reflected that not all maidens wore their hearts upon their sleeves.

Since I had paid off my debt to John Spare, and was laying by most of my earnings, and hoping for a better day, I had felt free to let my love for Eunice Spare grow unchecked; but I had not yet dared to show it, although I may have done so without knowing it. Theodore Morris had many advantages over me in winning her favor. He was first in the field, and he had ready at hand what I could only acquire slowly, try as I might. In his absence I was now restrained from saying anything in his disfavor, though I could have said a little. Face to face I had given him back cheerfully some of his own coin, according to the rules of sport, but while driving home that Sunday with Eunice, neither of us spoke further of him. She was free enough to talk of Theodore's father, and of his misfortune, and to say how humiliating it would be to him, and that she feared it would send him to bed ill, now that he was growing old and failing.

"Father," she continued, "is not as old as Judge Morris by ten years, but there is a greater difference than age. Father wouldn't be hurt by such a happening, but I fear that Judge Morris will be. Do you know, Richard Holt, I am right fond of Judge Morris, although he is so reserved, and some times so distant, and seems to be measuring and weighing you, both at the same time."

I did not mind at all how much Eunice Spare liked Theodore Morris's father, being only glad to have her seated at my side, talking prettily, and saying things which did her credit.

"Sometimes I have thought," she went on, "that if I were

in doubt, or in great trouble, or if I were old and about to die, and leave to somebody who was still a little girl a vast number of pounds from a pot of gold at the end of a rain-bow, there is nobody whom I would rather trust than Judge Morris, not even father."

"Why more than in your father?" I asked, having my curiosity aroused.

"Well, I don't know. Father has lived on a farm, and is wise about crops and the soil and cattle, and how to keep the weeds down, and what is best to be done at the school and the church, and whether prices will go up or down. And he knows whether men are to be trusted. You see he trusts Judge Morris, and I guess that is why I trust him."

She finished her reasoning suddenly, and we fell to wondering who the robber could be, but as Theodore had not told of Doane's letter, could make no guess, until John Spare brought home from the black-smith shop the hand-bills offering a reward for the detention of Moses Doane.

❧ 11 ❧

The Philler Vendue

I WROTE DOWN that it was in February, when the robber made his way into Judge Morris's house, and I think that it was. At the end of March a messenger brought a letter to John Spare, and I happened to be with him when it came. The messenger said that at the cross-roads, two or three miles away, a man on horse-back had asked him to carry the letter, and had given him a shilling for his trouble.

"I would ride all day for a shilling every two miles. The letter must be important," said John Spare, as he broke the seal, and sat down upon the well-curb. He read the letter through several times, and then we went on with our work, replacing some of the rotting planks about the well. On the next evening, after supper, when Mercy Spare and her niece had gone to their rooms, and we were smoking a last pipeful before going to bed, he said to me:

"Richard, I want you to go with me to the Philler vendue on Saturday morning."

I was much surprised, as I knew the Philler farm to be a run down place, where the hay crops were full of weeds, the cows under size, and the ploughs and harrows, waggons and tools were not of a quality to suit John Spare.

"I have had a strange letter," he continued, "I have thought it over, and decided to do what the writer asks me to do, to keep an appointment with a man—I don't know whom—about—I cannot guess what."

I was still more surprised by this, as it was not like John Spare to do anything except openly and above board. He went on:

"The writer of this letter—he signs himself 'Samuel Faunce' says that at eleven o'clock, when the people will be out in the barnyard, watching the sale of the cattle, he wants me to meet him on the barn floor, where the wheat bins are. He says that the entrance to the bins is through a door which can be closed to make all private and confidential. A very pretty letter to send to a churchman, Richard. What do you think?"

"It looks like plotting."

"It does, particularly as he says he will mingle with the crowd at first, and that I may know him by a hemlock switch which he will carry in his hand. Now, Richard, I want you to take a pistol, make your way at an early hour to some place overhead, where you can see and hear, and be ready if I need you."

On Saturday I found such a place unobserved easily enough in the haymow and when I had chosen it, and made sure that I could see down into the passage way along the wheat bins, I still had plenty of time to watch, through the spaces between the boards, the crowd in the barn yard, where the cattle were brought from their stalls. Many of the people assembled I did not know, but presently I saw William Barnes, Abel Strong and Stacey Claypoole, and after a while a man with his back towards me, bearing a hemlock branch in his hand. He was talking with someone whom at first I could not see. So I moved to a better look-out place, and saw in a minute that it was Jim Ferrell, and knew that mischief was in the wind, and I had best be careful. The knowledge sent me up to the haymow, and I took out my pistol, and had a long while to lie on the hay before anybody came in sight. It was warm and soft and quiet in the hay. I could hear faintly the droning of the voice of the auctioneer, who was David Wilkinson, the leader of our church choir. He was in great demand for the crying of our vendues because of his gift of setting one bidder against another, and starting rivalry, and often he would have a man bidding against himself, whereupon, when it was discovered by the crowd, there would be roars of laughter. From where I lay I could tell by the sound when David had been successful in this way, and was earning his pay by getting the best price possible.

Perhaps I slept, while losing my sense of duty in the comfort of the hay. Except in case of illness we farmers do not lie down until night, and then it is to sleep that we do it, and with us the position for slumber soon brings forgetfulness; but I was wide awake when there came to me up the funnel for chuting the hay from the mow down to the stables below the sound of two voices, one of which was saying:

"You think he'll be along about Friday afternoon of next week. Yes, I'll tell Bane. All will be done quietly and nobody will be the wiser."

This voice I did not recognize, never having heard it before to the best of my knowledge, and, as I have said before, my memory for the voice of a human being excels my memory of a human face. But Bane was the name of the tavern keeper of evil repute, and I thought that very likely the speaker was Jim Ferrell, whom I had seen oftener than I cared to see him, but had never heard speak. Then a second voice said:

"We must hurry, Jere, and get out of this. It's time for me to meet John Spare. You understand, Friday afternoon next. Tell Bane not to make any blunders or you'll both feel the halter."

I was now certain it was English Jim passing under his American name of Jerry; and the second voice I knew at once better than I knew my own. It was the voice of "The Dummy" of the fishing share and my bed fellow of the potato bags at The Bell tavern, the highwayman who possessed himself of John Spare's market money and substituted the bag of leaden discs in my great coat pocket. Some of that lead, melted down and moulded over, was now rammed home in my horse pistol, and much would I have liked to return it. I had almost rushed down to get a sight of the man when I remembered why I was in the haymow. So I lay down, with no inclination to go to sleep, on the edge of the hay above the wheat bins. It was a matter of fifteen or twenty minutes later that I heard the footsteps of two persons ascend the steps from the stable to the barn floor, and go around to the wheat bins, and looking down I saw John Spare and the man whose back I had seen in the barnyard. He still carried the hemlock branch, switching it jauntily against his leg. When the door was closed behind the two, he said in the voice which I remembered so well, and had just heard again at the foot of the hay funnel;

"Spare, I can't waste any time. You know who I am? No! I am Moses Doane. Make no sound. I mean you no harm."

As Doane spoke, he moved so that I saw his face plainly, and to my vast surprise, though his voice was the voice of the highwayman who rode in the waggon with me, the sight of his face threw me into a maze of doubt. The one man had dark hair and a pallid complexion. This man's hair was reddish, and his face was ruddy. I thought I should have known his eyes, but from my elevation could not see their color.

John Spare stood motionless and silent as if waiting for Doane to speak again. I could have shot Doane down, for quietly I had taken out my pistol, and my eye, glancing along the barrel, saw where his heart should be. Or, between us we could, perhaps, have made him prisoner, but feeling sure that John Spare had some valid reason for so strange a meeting, I durst not stir lest I spoil the plan, whatever it was.

"Spare, you and Judge Morris share a secret about your daughter, Eunice, which you do not want the world to know. Both of you think that you two alone know it. You mistake. I know it."

I could see that John Spare was startled by a movement of his body and a slight raising of his hands. He controlled himself, however, and Doane went on.

"You know best what my silence is worth to you. A week from today, at ten o'clock at night, at Bane's tavern, send me word what it is worth to you. Inquire for Mulford. Mulford! Don't forget the name. Good day."

Doane turned, and was gone so quickly that his departure startled me almost as much as his demand had taken me by surprise. I hurried down, and looked out on the barn yard, Doane was not there, I ran to the big door which faced the road, and saw going over the hill at a fast trot, on a black horse, a rider whom I did not doubt was Moses Doane.

John Spare and I walked home together over the muddy roads, and he was more perturbed than I had ever seen him. Things which he had always noticed he did not notice at all. One of the farm hands had left the bars down of our barn field, which was next the road, and he paid no attention. I put up the bars, and overtook him. He walked as if suddenly he had become tired. The only time he spoke was when nearing the house, he said,

"Richard, say nothing of this to any one. I will see what is to be done."

The next morning he said he must go to see Judge Morris. He was gone the better part of the day, and came home weary from the long horseback ride over the bad roads, and I thought disappointed. He told us that Judge Morris was ill, and in bed, that the presence of the robber in his house had done him more harm than at first had been thought, and he was unable to see any one. When I saw sturdy John Spare in this disturbed state, and looked upon his sister, Mercy, and daughter, Eunice, going about their usual occupation, unconscious of what had occurred, but with a sense of something gone wrong, I had the same feeling with which I had looked for the last time upon the horses and cows on our farm in England, and shivered from a shadow thrown upon me by the lack of substance and reality in life.

In the Spare homestead the foundations had seemed as firm as the eternal hills. A few words spoken by a highwayman, and though the Spare house, the Spare barn and the Spare fields were there as before, and would continue to be, nevertheless, the foundations were threatened. What mystery was this concerning Eunice Spare, a mystery known to a common footpad! What had two men like honest John Spare and Judge Morris agreed to conceal from the world? That there was something to be concealed, and that it was no trifling matter, John Spare's bearing since his return from the Philler vendue left no room for doubt. His silence continued day after day, and beyond questions made necessary by the farm work, I refrained from intruding upon his reticence. His daughter tried to maintain her usual good spirits, but a kind of gloom settled down upon us, and matters were not improved by Mercy Spare's ill-judged efforts to rouse us up.

"What ails you all?" she asked at the table. "Owls couldn't look more solemn or say less. You act as if you had heard dreadful news," and she would go on making me wince inwardly, and wish she would be still, like the rest of us. In the presence of her father, Eunice Spare kept up a pretence of not seeing that anything was wrong, but as she was going to the cave, where the butter and milk were now that winter was gone, and I was going the same way to the wood lot, she said to me:

"If father has any trouble, I am glad he intends to see Judge Morris. Father has not been like himself since he went to the Philler vendue. I wish you had been with him that day, instead of going off to the wheelwright's. I am sure he isn't ill. He must have heard something, that he is so upset."

On the morning of the vendue I had made the excuse of an errand to the wheelright's, and to ease my conscience had stopped to see what progress he was making with our new hay waggon, and thought I was well out of it. Now I was in again, as I had to let Eunice continue to think that I had not been with her father. If John Spare had heard something to upset him, I was in a worse state, because he knew what the trouble was, and I did not, and in my ignorance feared disgrace. Then I tried to drive such fears away. There could be nothing disgraceful where John Spare, Eunice Spare, and Judge Morris were concerned, and I felt better, until my doubts returned again, when I wished I knew all.

As the days went by John Spare's surprise wore off, and by Saturday he was used to Moses Doane's knowing a secret, which he had supposed was confined to Judge Morris and himself. When he had aught to say to me out of common, it was his habit to wait until his sister and daughter had gone upstairs for the night, and when Saturday evening came and I saw no signs of any message going to the tavern, as Doane had directed,

I thought if I was to learn anything of the business at hand that would be the time. Sure enough, when we two men were quiet together, he said:

"Richard, I can't think that Doane would trust himself to come back to this neighborhood so soon, with a reward over his head. He's a bold fellow, but hardly that bold. 'Mulford,' likely, would turn out to be one of his relations, not so well known as Doane himself. I'm not going to see 'Mulford,' whoever he is, or to send him any message. I wish I could have talked with Judge Morris. As it is, it's a puzzle to me. What disturbs me is to have that man and his fellows on my trail. He smells money and one way or another he will try to force money from me."

I had learned little, but it was enough to allay my fears. The secret, whatever it was, was not something that John Spare would seek to cover up by buying off the highwayman.

12

The Flood in the Branch

IN JUNE of that year the English army marched for the Jerseys, with the Americans after them. We could now go to the city market again, could sell our products once more, and could have seen our way to a fortune, if it had not taken so many of the paper bills to make up the worth of a few coins. There were no more American officers from the camp to come to our church on Sunday mornings, though there were both officers and soldiers who had died of wounds, and had been left in our church yard, or in the fields of some of the farms, but the living soldiers were all gone away, and we did not see them again while the war lasted.

In May, Theodore Morris had told us that his father was about once more, and much as usual, except that he did not seem strong, and John Spare had ridden over to see Judge Morris and did not return until the next day. What he learned he did not make known. Some months after this, in September, Eunice Spare came down stairs one morning very merry with a flower in her hair, which her father noticed, and smiled at.

"What day is this?" he asked as if he did not already know.

"Father!" she answered rebukingly. "Don't you remember? It's my birthday. I'll soon be an old maid. I'm getting ancient so fast. When Richard Holt came I was eighteen. That was four years ago, and it seems forever. How did we do before he came? I can scarcely remember, it was so long ago. But you are no older, father. Just stay as you are, and I'll catch up to you, and then we'll grow old together."

How quaint and pretty and whimsical she was in the light moods that came over her! Her father thought so too, but Mercy Spare said:

"No older! What nonsense child! When I was your age maids married at twenty, if they married at all, which I never did, and were mistresses of their own homes, and had much to manage, if they married well. I don't know what the maids now-a-days are thinking of."

"Aunt Mercy, how could a maid be thinking of marriage with a war going on, and robbers abroad, and the roads not safe? Not even a chance to buy pretty things to wear. Whom should I marry? David Wilkinson? He's far too old, and besides he never asked me. Maybe he will yet, and I'll think of him."

I knew that her aunt was not giving a thought to David Wilkinson, though I suspected that she gave more than one favorable thought to Theodore Morris. Having been a maid a long time herself, she knew the ways of maids, and forbore to say whom her niece might marry, if she chose.

"So you're twenty-two today, and in another year you'll be twenty-three."

"Will twenty-three be any more important than twenty-two? What will happen then, father?"

She was quick after a thought as a foxhound after a scent. Her father answered in a way that carried a meaning beyond the words.

"I heard of a maid once who was to be told something when she was twenty-three years old and not a moment before."

Eunice did not ask if she were to be told anything when she was twenty-three. She asked no question at all. Her air of banter changed, and a look of wonder passed over her face. After breakfast I heard her singing at her work, her voice growing fainter, and stopping in the middle of a bar. Then she sang a bar or two more, and was still again, until I had to go to the fields and was out of hearing. I thought that John Spare considered how, if anything happened to him now that the Doanes were threatening, he would not leave his daughter, who was dearer to him than anybody else, without a hint as to what he knew. He could not tell her; but if he gave her a hint, and any harm befell him, it would be a word to her from beyond his grave and she would understand.

The departure of the armies in June had opened a wider region for the Doanes to work in, and their daring and successes drew to them a number of men who liked the freedom of the life, and an easy way of acquiring riches. Clear from one river to the other, they struck, now here, and now there, never twice in the same section, and some of their followers, becoming brutal with practice, not sparing the women in their later exploits as they had in the beginning. As rumors of their robberies, attacks on homes and even burnings of dwellings, reached us, we began to wonder if we should escape their attentions, especially as John Spare had not met Moses Doane or his messenger according to expectations. That is, John Spare and I wondered. His sister and daughter had only the general knowledge of the Doanes which everybody had.

It had been in June that another letter had come to John Spare. I found it in the early morning, in the oats box, on top of the grain, when I went to feed the horses, and it had not been there the evening before. This letter contained a threat, not saying whether murder or house firing was in store for us, but leaving that to us to make out as best we could. We cleaned the fire arms again, and took turns for a while watching at night; but as nothing happened, and watching was wearing, and the hay would soon be fit to mow, we took to our beds again, but not with confidence, or with a feeling of freshness in the morning. I have heard city people say that country life lacked excitement, and there was nothing to talk about. It was not that way with us. The last thing at night, I looked out of the window for signs of fire. If John Spare went over the hill alone, or beyond the woods, I wondered what to do if he never came back. In my sleep there came a persistent dream that the Doanes had forced their way into the choir loft, and with pistols leveled commanded David Wilkinson to sing a drinking song. So that night and day we had the Doanes on our minds, and they kept us from growing dull, if that had been possible where Eunice Spare was.

Then, unexpectedly, there came a period of security. It began to rain, and continued raining, day after day and every night for more than a week. We could not go off the farm by way of the creek on one side, or by the branch on another, because the streams were over their banks, and running too swiftly for a horse to swim. In a third direction was still another water course, which was now an impassable torrent, so that but one narrow exit was left to us, and that led nowhere. If we could not leave the farm, neither could anyone reach us, without a journey of many miles, and we stopped thinking about the Doanes, and waited for the waters to go down, when the mowers could come, and help us with the hay harvest. Still, it was better that the grass should be standing, than that it should be lying on the ground to spoil, with all the trouble of turning it, and no sun to dry the hay.

On the fourth or fifth day of the rainy week, the clouds lifted for an hour or more, not to clear off, for the wind was still in the East, but to pile up in hillocks in the sky. Eunice and I walked across the sodden fields to the high ground bordering on the branch, and looked down on the discolored waters, which were leaping and plunging like troops of wild horses. On the surface was hurled along all manner of debris from the farms above, and the noise was so great that, with the roar of the wind, we had to speak loudly to make ourselves heard. At the highest point of land Eunice could scarcely make headway against the wind, and took my arm until we descended the steep bank a little, and found a place of shelter. On the opposite shore rose a sheer wall of rock of many warm colors to the height of a hundred feet, and on the ledges of this wall, where soil had lodged, were growths of hemlocks and cedar; and the curve of the stream was such that the waters, leaping against the base of the precipice were thrown high in the air; and rails and planks, striking an obstacle, leaped clear out of the water, to plunge again for a moment out of sight. We had stood there for as much as fifteen minutes in silence, all thought of speech being taken away by the sight of the flood's power, when Eunice grasped my arm, and said:

"Richard! Look, quick! What is that?"

Towards us on the flood floated a pile of brush and drift-wood, on which lay a huddle of clothing, with a bright color showing, which might hide a child. Fifty yards down the stream there was an eddy, before the current narrowed and leaped forward again at a swifter rate. I had seen that at this eddy all things adrift, drawn into it, circled about several times before they were swept onward again, and the low branches of the trees, their trunks surrounded with water, reached well out towards the margin of the eddy. As fast as I could, I made my way to this place, and was out in the water, waist deep, with a firm hold on an over-hanging limb by the time the pile of brushwood with its burden was drawn into the eddy. At first the force of the current above shot the fragile raft across the edge, and to the center of the eddy, and it was beyond my reach, strive as hard as I could, without letting go the tree limb, to grasp one branch after another projecting from the floating pile, and much I feared, if I succeeded, that I might pull out a sustaining plank or rail and cause the whole to fall apart, like a pile of jack straws.

I had time to think of this danger when the pile lost speed, as it approached the lower arc of the circling eddy, and still more slowly started to come back on the circumference up the circling waters again, precisely as I hoped it would from the way the waters were at play there. Once started, it went all the way around the edge, and when it came by me a second time, it was within the reach of my arm, and though fearful lest the limb to which I clung, should break, or my feet be swept from under me, I managed to lay a firm grasp on the bundle, and bore it ashore, while the raft went on its journey. At once, at the touch, I knew it was a child. Eunice Spare had run along the bluff, and made her way down the steep descent by the time I reached the shore with my burden. She drew back the garment which hid the child's face, but whether it was drowned or living, or a boy or a girl, I could not tell.

"I believe he's alive! I believe he's alive! Hurry, Richard!"

Now, my wet clothing clung to me. My shoes were full of water. The steep was hard to climb with the child in my arms; and, in the fields, the ground was soft. So, it seemed a slow pace with which we reached the house, and I had time to notice that Eunice was panting with excitement, to remember that she had called me Richard, without adding my surname, as had been her habit, which I thought might have been for lack of time, and to wonder how she had known that the pallid face and closed eyes were those of a boy and not of a girl. Mercy Spare saw us coming as we neared the house, my wet clothing and the child in my arms, and said excitedly:

"God bless us! What has happened?"

"A half-drowned baby, Aunt Mercy! Richard drew it from the flood. Hurry, Aunt Mercy!"

I carried the child up the stairs, Mercy Spare making no protest against the soiling of the floors from my dripping garments. While Eunice brought hot water and flannels, her aunt took off the child's wet clothing, and I left him in their hands. What with the warmth, the rubbing, a little spirits and hot broth, in a few hours something of his natural color returned; the blood came back to his hands and feet, and he slept in a way that showed that he was doing as well as could be hoped for, though it was several days before he was on his feet again, and then his legs were only good for a step or two. The child was barely seven years old, a pretty boy, as we saw when he came to himself, and when he was not lying in his cot asleep, he liked mostly to be held in Eunice Spare's lap. Of an evening, I whittled out two or three toys for him, and he held one of these tightly in each hand as he fell asleep. The rest of us were slow to win his confidence, but Eunice found her way to this heart at once, so that he was not content when she was away from him. Much of her time she now spent in fashioning clothing for him, his mud-soaked and shrunken garments having to be discarded. When he was strong enough, and had grown accustomed to us, and had got so that he would say bravely, when offered food, that he liked this or did not like that, and showed an interest in everything, she tried to find out what his name was. Handing a top to him, she asked:

"Whose horse is this?"

"Mine," he answered, confidently.

"What is the horse's name?"

"Toby."

"What is my name?"

"Oonice."

"What is your name?"

But she got no reply, nor ever could. We thought his silence a passing whim, but had no better success when by different ways we thought at intervals to surprise him. Neither could we discover how far or for how long a time he had drifted in the flood, or whether, wandering off to the water's edge, he had been fascinated by the flood, ventured too close, and been swept away. We learned that four or five persons had been drowned in that great flood, some by trying to save floating property, and others while attempting to cross the streams with horses or boat, and two of these bodies were carried ten miles down the creek to the river, and were not recovered until changed beyond recognition.

One day, after Eunice had tried all the given names that she knew that are born by males, without the child's giving a sign of response, she said:

"We shall have to call him Eddie Waters, from the eddy in the waters where we found him," and so we did for want of a better name, though at first we smiled at the conceit.

He turned out to be a sturdy boy, and of an inquiring turn of mind, shown by his wanting to follow Eunice to the cave, or me to the barn, or even to the fields, when I would have to turn him around and give him a start towards Eunice, watching from the house.

After the rain stopped falling, the sky cleared with a period of great heat, during which the low fields gave off a vapor that took the heart out of a man for hard work. Nevertheless, we went at the hay, and the mowers began to arrive as the flood went down, all of them with tales of the high water, until they heard our story of the rescued boy, when they wanted to see him, not because they doubted us, but out of natural curiosity. Though many saw him now, none of them had seen him before, so we got no help in this direction, though the men could be depended upon to spread the word.

With the abundant rains, we had the greatest crop of hay that year that I ever saw out on the farm. The mows would not hold it, and we made as many as three or four ricks outside, and in the field there was, besides, a row of hay-cocks waiting to be loaded on the hay waggon. As I have said before, Eunice Spare liked to drive the hay waggon, after it was loaded, from the field to the barn, and to go through the bars without striking either post, and along the slope without overturning the load, and up the berm-bank, knowing just when to duck the head under the door frame called for some skill, and no wonder if Eunice, perched on top of the hay load, with the long lines in her hands, felt a glow of pride as she heard the clatter of the horses' feet on the barn floor. On Friday afternoon she had brought the boy out to the hay field, and put him in care of one of the loaders on top of the load of hay while she drove to the barn. Nor was he much in the way. In the field he toddled along after the waggon until it was loaded and driven by Eunice to the bars, where, by standing on the top rail of the fence, I could take the boy from a loader, who would say, "Up with you, my man!" and pass him to another on top of the hay. Then Eunice gave him the slack of the lines to hold, and very earnestly he held them. So he rode until supper time, so full of consequence and happiness that he did not want to stop work, and all the men laughed, asking him if he'd have them work all night.

At the supper table he had his bread and milk, and slipped out of his high chair, one that John Spare had himself used when of the same age. It was dusk when we had finished eating, and Mercy Spare went to fetch the boy to put him to bed, but he was nowhere to be found. It was Eunice who said:

"Richard, I believe he has gone to the hay field again."

And I went to find him. He was not in the field, and I went to the barn whose big doors stood wide open. By this time there was barely light enough to see out of doors, and within the barn, objects could scarcely be discerned. The barn floor was empty, except for the unloaded hay waggon. Next I went to the one hay rick, which we had put up by that time, of poorer hay that was mixed with weeds. Coming out of the barn, I could see better, now, under the sky, and walking hurriedly around the rick to the further side, stood face to face with three armed men, one of whom held the boy I was looking for close to his breast. Not being prepared for such a sight, I was greatly taken aback, and knew not what to say, and if I had known, little difference would it have made. A voice, which instantly I knew to be that of Moses Doane, said in a commanding tone:

"Holt, how came this boy here?"

Now why it should be Moses Doane's business to know the particulars of the child's rescue was not clear to me, and I did not reply promptly, whereupon I heard a pistol cocked as if to enforce the query. At the instant, too, it came to me that the child was on good terms with the men, and perhaps they knew more about him than I did, which was little enough, so I said in turn:

"What right have you to ask?"

"The right of kin. The boy is my brother's son. We thought him drowned."

Knowing well by this time Doane's custom of pretending to be what he was not, I might not have believed him except for the conduct of the child, which bore in upon me a thought that the robber for once might be speaking the truth, and therefore I said:

"Moses Doane, you robbed me once. For all I know you may be lying to me now as you did before. How am I to know?"

"Ask the boy," he answered, taking him from the other man's arms and leading him to me, "ask him now what you please." To my questions the boy answered in a sleepy voice that father and uncle had come to take him home. "Now," I said, "tell me your name," and without any hesitation he replied:

"Joey Doane."

When I considered how he would never tell us before, I was forced to believe that he had been taught not to reply to the question when strangers asked it, and that he was a true scion of the stock, and competent for one of his years. Briefly then to the father and uncle and the third man I told how we had seen the child floating on the flood, and I had managed to rescue him half-drowned, and never been able to get into my shrunken clothes or shoes since, and that the women with hard work had restored him to life, and I hoped he would grow up to be an honest man.

"Furthermore," I said, "we have been right glad to have him about, and Eunice Spare will miss the boy, now you have come for him."

"We did not come for him," said Moses Doane, "but we will take him with us. We came for something else. That we will not take. Say to John Spare that his house or his barn will never be burned, nor his horses, his cattle, his crops, raided or taken by a Doane. Tell him that the roads will be safe for him and his."

Whistling shrilly on something which he took from his pocket, he called to him from the darkness two mounted men, who rode near with three led horses, and the father, taking the boy, now fast asleep in his arms, all turned their horses, and disappeared without a word more, and I thought the going of the waif as sudden as his coming.

When I returned to the house, thinking how I should tell them, the candles were lit, and Mercy Spare was waiting to put the boy to bed. Then the women saw me without him; for the first time they were alarmed.

"Fetch the lanthorn, daughter," said John Spare. "He's fallen asleep somewhere."

"No," I said, "he's gone."

"Gone! Gone where?"

"His father and uncles and others, five of them in all, came and took him with them. His name is Joey Doane, and he knew it well enough all the time."

"Lord save us," said Mercy Spare, "five of the Doanes here, and no harm come of it!"

Then I told them what had happened, and what had been said, and how Moses Doane had learned about our saving the boy's life, and nursing him back to health, and how he bade me tell John Spare that no harm would come to him or to his from any Doane, neither at home or abroad.

"He said they would not burn?" John Spare asked.

"Yes."

"Nor steal any cattle?"

"Yes."

"And we could go and come without being molested?"

"All that he said."

"Then we know what they had in mind to do, and what we have escaped. You think he said this because we did what any Christian would have done?"

"Not a doubt of it."

"Richard, I have known long that good men are not all good. It may be that bad men are not all bad."

❧ 13 ❧

Job Tully's Warning

FOR SO LONG A TIME had we gone about with no comfort, and with much looking over our shoulders, and to bed with uncertainty, that our new freedom was as if a weight had been lifted from us. We had felt shut in, and now the landscape was spread out before us, and we could go where we wished. Then a new discomfort took the place of that which we had been glad to part with. We were burdened with a new secret. If we boasted of our good fortune, it would show to our neighbors how much better off we were than they, and jealousy is a rank weed, hard to uproot when once started. Not knowing what to say, we said nothing, or as little as possible. The passing curiosity of the mowers about the disappearance of Joey Doane was easily satisfied by telling them that his people had come for him, and they would think no more about him, as long as they did not know that he was a Doane. But as we began to go about—to market in the city, to church, here and there, wherever the need was, freely and with no precautions against danger, this freedom of movement soon caused comment.

One Sunday morning the cows broke into the grain field, and Mercy and Eunice Spare went to church alone, as it was now safe for them to do. The next Sunday John Spare and I were taken to task for recklessness, and we were hard pressed not to set about proving that there was no recklessness in it. Theodore Morris had escorted the women all the way to our house in order to keep off the highwaymen, and he stayed to dinner. Not one of us dared to tell him of our new safety, and after that it was harder than ever to explain, and let him know how he had been deceived, which had not been intended. Eunice was distrait in his presence, as I had never seen her before, and we were all ill at ease through trying not to show it. He did not stay long, and after he had gone we began to see complications, and John Spare said that he was minded to make a clean breast of it.

That afternoon Eunice and I, with the two boys, walked to the branch, which was now so shallow that in places it could be waded across. Showing how high the waters had been, on the banks was a deposit of refuse left by the flood. While the boys were busy with throwing sticks into the water, and presently took off their shoes and began to wade in the stream, Eunice and I sat in the shade, until it was time to look after the cattle.

"Richard," she asked, "could the people blame you for taking Joey Doane from the flood, or father for giving him shelter, or Aunt Mercy and me for nursing him?"

"I hope not, Eunice."

"If they do, I shall hate them all. Anybody who would condemn us, if he had seen Joey Doane out yonder in a swirl of waters, where I first saw him or down below by the tree, where you drew him out—see how far above the water that tree is now, Richard?—why he would have let him drown without knowing whether it was a Doane floating by or somebody else. Richard, I was afraid you would be swept away. Once, my heart was in my mouth."

"If I had been swept away, Eunice?"

"If you had been swept away, we shouldn't have sheltered a little highwayman. He's too pretty to grow up to be a highwayman, Richard. And then our neighbors wouldn't be growing suspicious, and I might be here alone today, looking mournfully at the spot where Richard Holt went down. But that is silly, Richard. When I stood here in fright lest you be carried away, I prayed to our Father in Heaven for your safety. T'was He who helped you save the child."

She said this so simply and naturally that as I thought of

her standing on the brink of the flood, there was no room for any image of myself in the picture formed in my mind.

Suddenly she asked, "Wouldn't it be better, Richard, to tell the people why we can go about unprotected?"

"In ordinary times, yes. But now men's minds lay hold of small things, and put this and that together, and hold hard fast to their opinions."

"Let them," she exclaimed. "What matters it to us!"

"Eunice, if the people knew we had only talked to the Doanes, they would suspect us. If they thought the robbers were protecting us, they would be sure something was going on to help the English cause. Have you forgotten that I am an Englishman? My presence in your father's house would confirm suspicions. Then, too, Theodore Morris is friendly with you, and the Morrises, father and son, are well known to be Tory in their sympathy. I can see that it is something for your father to think well over."

The boys wearied of their play, and now rejoined us when we talked of other things, as we walked homewards.

I think, if John Spare had been left alone, he would have told his neighbors all about what had occurred, hoping that they would see it in the right light. They had not left him alone, but made him and all of us the subject of gossip, and he was not the man to act under pressure. At the mill, where I had taken a small grist to be ground, I came upon Job Tully and Walter Heacock, and as I drove up, I heard Heacock say:

"Here comes Holt, now. Ask him about it."

As I approached them, Tully said with some show of warmth:

"Holt, I want to know what that damned Tory, Theodore Morris, is prowling around here for at night. Heacock saw him on Monday night. Stackhouse met him at his lane on Wednesday night, and I passed him Saturday night, near Bane's tavern, riding like an express. What would the damned Tory be at?"

In jest I answered, "Maybe he's out courting."

Tully was known to be persistent in the courting of Annie

Bates, though so far without much success. He was not now in a jesting humor, and even in the best of moods, was more apt to quarrel and bluster than to laugh.

"I don't know where he would go courting around here, unless it's at John Spare's house," he said.

"Well, Tully, he hasn't been at John Spare's house but twice in two years to the best of my knowledge."

"May be he doesn't go to the house."

I was angry at this, and replied with heat:

"Tully, it's none of my business where he goes, and I don't believe it's any of yours," and I turned on my heel, when he shouted after me:

"He's a Tory, by God, and you're an Englishman! There's more than me putting two and two together, when you can ride the roads, and everybody else afeared to stir from home. John Spare had best be careful."

I knew that I could throw Job Tully into the next field, if I had a mind to, and, therefore could put up with his rough way of blurting out what I felt was the truth about the neighborhood suspicions. Indeed, what I had heard was little more than what I, myself, had said to Eunice, and I let it pass. On returning home, I repeated to John Spare what Tully had said, and thought from his reception of it that the outlook for public explanations was not promising. He was not a pretentious man, but he was a proud man, and where mere pretention would have broken down before opposition, he was like a rock, unchanged and unchangeable.

The next time we were at church, there were plainly to be seen signs of aloofness on the part of a number of the congregation. It had been the custom, as we came to the church door, to exchange greetings with those persons who had already arrived, with much shaking of hands and many inquiries about friends who were ill, or absent for some other cause. But on this Sunday a number failed to greet us, either before or after the service.

David Wilkinson was not a bold man, but all for smoothing things over. It was like him to be as friendly as ever in manner, and yet show that he held something in reserve.

"David," I said, "what has come over the people? Nobody has the pox at the Spare farm."

David never liked to be brought up squarely to a direct question, and still less did he like to give a direct answer, and rather than do it, he would agree with you a long way, or at any rate not contradict you, though he was as honest as most men. Now, he boxed the compass to see which way lay the smoothest water, but I would not let him off so easily.

"Tell me, David, what is wrong?"

Seeing no way out, at last, reluctantly, he said that Adam Supplee, the crabbed vestryman, had expressed to members of the vestry disapproval of my singing in the choir.

"Doesn't he like the way I sing, David?"

"Bless me! Nothing so bad as that. But he says you are an Englishman, only a few years here, and he suspects you would like to pray for the king."

"No doubt the king, like other men, needs praying for, David. But what did the vestrymen say?"

Some of them agreed with Adam, and some didn't. Some thought it would be better if you withdrew from the choir, as Judge Morris did from the vestry because he was a Tory."

"Do they say that I am a Tory, David?"

"They say—"but David thought that he had revealed too much already. I got no more from him, but for what he had told me, I gave him something to think about.

"David, Adam Supplee is a narrow, un-Christian-like bigot. Nevertheless, I shall not sing in the choir again until I am asked."

At the dinner table I announced this decision to the family, when the matter was made to appear in a new light by John Spare. Abel Strong had told him that Jeremiah, the hostler at Bane's tavern, or Jim Ferrell as I knew him, had been hinting to several persons that the Spares were having meetings with the Doanes, and that was the reason why we were now so bold on the highways. When this intelligence had been conveyed to Abel Strong with some additions, he had said:

"Of course that shuffle-jointed rascal is lying."

But John Spare and I had met Moses Doane at the vendue,

and I had met him twice more, once when he robbed me, and again behind the hay stack, and we had the Doane promise and were living up to it, as the Doanes were, too, in a very creditable way. What with John Spare's consciousness of our virtue, and his pride aroused, and his indignation that his neighbors should fall away from him for no just cause, I saw no way out.

When Eunice heard what David Wilkinson had told me, and what Abel Strong had repeated to her father, she declared that neither would she sing in the choir more, until I was asked to return, but would sit with her father and her aunt Mercy in the pew, and her aunt Mercy announced that she would not go to our church at all until the manners improved, but to the Mennonite meeting house, where the preaching was sometimes in Dutch but generally in German, of which tongues she knew but a word or two.

The following Sunday Mercy Spare stayed at home, Eunice and I sat in her father's pew, and heard what the choir singing sounded like from a distance. Annie Bates was really grieved, and David Wilkinson looked as if he were sorry, but it could not be helped.

14

John Spare In Trouble

WHILE THE ARMIES were in our section of the country, and battles were fought, people lost interest in the disappearance of the cattle dealers. All that time the civil powers were in a measure helpless. Now they began to assert themselves again. The sheriffs of three counties set about running down the Doanes, but so far their net had brought in nothing. Several times we met on the road strange men, and we heard that constables from the city were exploring our neighborhood, asking questions, and that they had paid repeated visits to Bane's tavern, and had been seen talking with the hostler. Being cut off now from the good feeling which had formerly enabled us to hear what was going on, we missed a good deal. Otherwise we should not have been taken so much by surprise by what happened.

Early one morning, John Spare and I were on our way to the fields, when we saw two men riding up the lane, one of whom I had met on the roads without knowing his business. We waited for the strangers to draw near. The older of the two dismounted, while the other held his horse, and approaching said;

"Your name is John Spare, isn't it?"

"Yes, I am John Spare."

"I have a warrent for your arrest," and at once he began to read in a monotonous voice, as if he never did anything else but read such documents, and the novelty had departed, a paper full of large words with a seal attached, commanding him to take into custody the person of John Spare, and deliver him to the gaoler at Philadelphia.

"On what charge?" John Spare asked, "I did not hear."

"On the charge of aiding and abetting. You'll find out soon enough. Let's see!" and he took out his watch. "I'll give you an hour to get ready."

I saddled the horses. Eunice tearfully packed her father's saddle bags, and her aunt told the men what she thought of them, but they were used to it, and all her talk made no difference in our going. In less than an hour we were on our way. I told John Spare that I would do the best I could with the farm work, parted from him at the gaol door, and at dark was back home with the led horse. Eunice and her aunt were watching for me; the table was spread, and John Spare's arm chair was drawn up to its place, where it remained unoccupied. I tried to comfort them by saying that the truth would soon be known, and he would be free again, but it was a dreary time. So far as I knew, I told them all the ins and outs of the matter, some of which they had not heard before, but something remained, which none of us knew, which was why John Spare had gone to the Philler vendue, and talked with Moses Doane, and afterwards had ridden twice to see Judge Morris, the last time staying all night.

"Ye shan't know all until I am twenty-three," said Eunice. "You remember what father said on my birthday about a maid who was to be told something when she was twenty three, and not a moment before. I am the maid, and because father cannot tell now he has to go to gaol."

"Eunice, be sensible," said her aunt. "Your father could tell about Richard's saving Joey Doane's life, and the Doanes coming to take the boy, and telling us that they would let us alone."

"So he could, Aunt Mercy, but would that explain why father went to the Philler vendue with Richard, and talked in the barn with Moses Doane, unless father made it known that there was a secret, which Doane had got wind of. Father isn't ready to make that known, and somebody has told that father talked with Moses Doane."

Then I thought of Jim Ferrell. I had overheard him talking

with Doane, when I lay in the hay-mow of the Philler barn on the day of the vendue, and there, I thought, is the clue to John Spare's arrest on nothing at all. Jim Ferrell, who was in some plot, as was clear from what I had overheard between him and Moses Doane—Jim Ferrell, who was a rascal through and through, and could be loyal to nobody, was now playing false to the Doanes, and putting the constables on the scent with a notion of saving his own neck when the time came. It would be natural for him to think that John Spare's meeting with a Doane could be for no honest purpose, and I thought I saw how he had used what he had learned. I waited for a chance to tell Eunice what had come to me because of her remark, for I was afraid that her aunt, in her indignation, would blurt it all out, before the time was ripe for it. What with all the work, and the responsibility, and John Spare's two boys in need of company to console them for their father's absence, the opportunity to talk alone with Eunice did not come until late the next day, when I said to her:

"How to lay hold of Jim Ferrell is something I cannot make out."

"Richard, would the hostler go directly to the constable, and tell him what he knew?"

"No, he wouldn't. He would be afraid. The constable would ask him where he learned this, and Jim would have to invent something, or say he was with Moses Doane himself, and he'd fear to get entangled. No, he would send a dirty, unsigned note that the constable could hardly read, or some such way."

"Richard, if the Doanes thought that Jim Ferrell had betrayed them, wouldn't they want to entrap him?"

I had never thought of that. Besides, the more intimate we were with the Doanes, the more trouble we got into. Though I was reluctant from fearing that I might be the next to be clapped into gaol, the thought which Eunice had put forth came back to me again and again. At the same time I was dwelling on another plan to help John Spare, and the next day I rode over to see what Judge Morris had to submit on the problem, it being in his line. The heat increased rapidly as the sun mounted higher, and as I neared the river the heavy clouds of a thunder storm darkened the western sky, and I rode rapidly to escape the coming rain. Judge Morris sat on his porch as I rode up, and a colored boy led my horse away to shelter. I approached the aging man with some misgivings. Had it been my own affair I had hardly dared to approach him at all. He might not remember me away from the church, the only place he had ever spoken to me. I told him my name, but he said in a kindly tone,

"I know you very well. And how is my friend, John Spare?"

This was bringing up the subject sooner than I had expected, and caused me to fear making too sudden a reply.

"In body, he was very well when I left him, but he is in sore trouble, and his sister and daughter are in a worse state of mind."

"John Spare in trouble! John Spare! What is it? What is it?"

Without more ado I laid before him the whole situation, and what led up to it. When he understood that John Spare was at that moment in the city gaol, his eyes glared, and his face turned red in a way to marvel at and his hand, holding his cane, shook, and he struck his stick sharply on the stone.

"Richard, you are of English birth?"

"Yes, only an American for four years."

"You won't repeat what I am going to say to my disadvantage. You need not promise, I will trust you. My fellow Americans are new to government. Mostly, they do not come from the governing class. They muddle things, as Richard Bentley said Epicurus did. Of course they have muddled this affair, and I fear, if they gain independence, they will go on muddling more serious things for two hundred years, growing more incompetent in government as the novices come more and more into power. Government calls for experience and knowledge, Richard."

I reflected that farming did, and surveying did. Perhaps government did. I did not know, and was silent. The old man then returned to the matter in hand.

"It will not do to have it appear that I am lifting a hand in John Spare's behalf. That would harm him more than help. But, Richard, I have still left two good American friends of the other party, men of substance, I will ask them to go to the city, and go on John's bail bond. It won't be refused. As soon as Theodore comes home, I will send him to see them. He will arrange for them to go to the city on Monday. On Tuesday, about sundown, meet John Spare with a second horse at the Fatland ford road, on your side of the river. If he fails to come on Tuesday, be there again Wednesday evening."

It all appeared very simple, and soon over, and I rose to thank him and depart.

"Wait a minute, I have something for you." Entering the house he brought back, and handed me a printed pamphlet without any backs.

"Take this with you, and study it," he said, "It will help you in your surveying."

I found that it was David Rittenhouse's method of correcting errors in observations, and for computing areas by double meridian distances. In the state of public feeling against us, I had ample time to study this new method of surveying before there was work offered me in which to practise it. By the old man's attention to a young man I was enabled to become one of the earliest of practical surveyors to put in use the method, which became widely known as the Pennsylvania method. Mercy and Eunice Spare were all eagerness to hear my story on my return, and rejoiced with me at the outcome of my visit to Judge Morris.

"I knew he could set father free, if anybody could," Eunice said, her face aglow with a new cheerfulness. And then:

"O, Richard, I almost forgot. There is a letter for you," and she went to fetch it. The address was written with flourishes of the pen made by no unskilled hand, which was unknown to me. Breaking the wax, I read an unsigned request in the same clear and careful hand, to meet the writer under the Black Oak tree, at the cross roads, on the next night at nine o'clock without fail, when I would hear of something to my advantage.

I asked Eunice who had brought the letter. She said it had been given to one of the farm hands while he was setting a fence post along the main road. She had asked who gave it, but the man who brought it to the house had not known. Here was another mystery letter to come to us and it smelled of trouble. Nevertheless, as it held out the hope of something to my advantage, I decided to see what it might be, and when the time came, went with caution on foot, starting as soon as it was dark.

Leaving the road four or five hundred yards from the meeting place, I skirted around by way of the fields, and entered the rear of a woods, through which I could make my way unseen close enough to learn whether the writer of the note, whoever he might be, was keeping his appointment, and whether he had brought anybody with him. I thought if he were alone, I would consider listening to what he had to tell me. If he were not alone, I would think further about it, and could retire through the woods, if I wished, and nobody the wiser. Sure enough, under the light of the moon, now in its second quarter, stood a man in the road by the side of his horse, and no one else in sight. So I approached to within a safe distance, and paused. The man by the horse gave a grim laugh.

"Holt," he said, "you come by the back way."

"Yes," I answered, "Formerly, I was all for openness, but my nature has changed."

"Then you are growing like other men. Most of us have two natures in these times, and first we show one, and then another, according to the persons we are with."

I was still on one side of the fence, and he on the other, and before crossing over I considered that it would be well to learn which one of his natures he intended to display to me. He appeared to be in no hurry to reveal himself, and as for me the moonlight would hold for some time yet.

"Holt, you are wondering why I am standing on the road, and you are over there in the field at this hour of night. We couldn't be where we are on a finer night, could we? How beautiful is that bar of cloud across the moon! How peaceful! Not a jarring sound! While waiting for you—you were ten minutes late, time lost in coming by way of the woods—as I stood here, seeing only the moonlight and the shadows, and hearing only the Katydids, I recalled such a night many years ago, when I was a lad and my mother heard my evening prayer, and the life about us was as peaceful as this moonlight scene. There came back to me Drummond's lines, I haven't thought of them since I left school, and it came over me that if we were indeed not foolish children, as the poet declares us to be, we might—

> 'Find out His power which wildest powers doth tame,
> His providence extending everywhere,
> His justice, which proud rebels doth not spare.' "

Discourse such as this was not according to my expectations, and with my lately acquired caution where the way was not clear, I misdoubted whither it would lead.

"Do you think," I queried, "that Master Drummond's lines have any bearing on the Americans, who are called by some Rebels, and by others Patriots."

"I was not thinking of them. I was thinking of proud natures that are made rebellious by oppression, as my brothers have been, as I have been. Think you, the Doanes follow the road from choice! 'Tis not so. Their enemies drove them to it."

When Judge Morris had quoted to me a saying of Richard Bentley, it came from him naturally, because he was a scholar, and familiar with the thoughts of scholars, but I had never looked for a Doane to talk sweetly, as this Doane was now talking by the roadside in the moonlight. In a way I was glad to gather that he was a Doane and feeling safe under the promise given us, I crossed the fence and stood by him. He had taken off his hat, and the moon falling fair upon his face, showed it to be stern and set, not a changeable face like that of his brother, Moses, not one indicating a man who could be all things to all men, but rather a man who though he might change sides, would be much the same on either side. He was broad of shoulder, powerful of limb and stood very erect, carrying his head high, tall, with his chest thrown out. I still waited patiently for him to explain why we were met under the Black Oak tree, having no doubt that he would make himself clear in good time, and I began to surmise that he was one of those men who, however determined and decisive in action, defer telling what they have to tell to the last moment, reluctant to part with their knowledge from a kind of acquisitiveness, and dwelling on many irrelevant matters, before they reach the pith of the subject. So I waited.

"There was Abraham, and Mahlon, and Moses, and I, who am Joseph, and our two sisters, all children in our father's house together, and father and mother were Friends in good standing in the meeting. Our home was a pleasant one by the spring, where the willows grew, and we had the warmth of simple fare, and the comfort of suitable clothing. We went to school, and I learned to write a good hand, and the schoolmaster said that I would make a scholar with opportunity. Father brought me books from the city, and I learned more than most knew of mathematics and history, and that I might have money to buy more books, when I was fit, I taught a school, and sometimes would have a pupil, who would be ambitious to write as fair a hand as I, myself, could write, because of possessing a sense of grace and symmetry in form. Then, because we stood by England's rights, our neighbors turned from us, and informed on us, made false charges against us, and persecuted as peaceful a household as there was in the three counties, or in America. One thing led to another, and now we are hunted from pillar to post, with no safe place to lay our heads, with every man's hand against us. Richard Holt, whatever you hear of the Doanes, I tell you, now, that the wrong is not all on our side. I have never struck, except to pay back an injury, or when my life was in danger. Sometimes, my brothers have gone too far, and sometimes, things have been laid at their door unfairly. Woe is me! These are wicked days. I long for the old peace and order."

I thought that Joseph Doane had become almost unaware of my presence, when in another tone, and without more of philosophy or poetry, or casting of the mind backward, he said:

"My brother, Moses, desired to see you himself, but he is too well known to appear in this neighborhood. I have come in his place. He told you that all of the members of the Spare household were safe from the Doanes, whether at home or abroad. There is something more. He sends you this." And he handed me a parcel of some weight. "Moses has sent this to you," he repeated, "I am only the carrier."

I now thought it time to bring forward what Eunice Spare had put into my mind, but which had been driven out of it by the unexpected meeting with the one member of the Doane family most likely to help us in the way Eunice had thought of.

"Joseph Doane," I asked, "do you know that John Spare is now locked up in the city gaol?"

He seemed almost as much surprised as Judge Morris had been, and he asked the same question which John Spare had asked when he was taken up.

"On what charge?"

"On the charge of aiding and abetting the Doanes."

His grim laugh broke out for an instant, and then he asked if I suspected any one of being the informer of such a falsehood. When I answered that I did, but had little to go by, and was not certain, he pressed me for the name, and I told him that I suspected the hostler called Jerry at Bane's tavern.

"Why do you say that he is called, Jerry?"

"Because I know that once he bore another name."

Joseph Doane blew the air out between his pursed lips without making a whistle, and then said:

"I have far to ride. It is time for me to go, I have had no dealings with Jerry by that or any other name. I will talk to Moses, do nothing until you hear from us," and he put his foot in the stirrup. His horse started forward at a sudden sound from both directions on the road, the animal's motion carrying Doane, as it will carry riders who know the trick, straight into the saddle.

"Quick, Richard, make for the woods. My two sentries are coming. That means the hunt is up."

I gained the shadows of the near woods, and turned to see Doane sitting quietly upon his horse, while from each direction on the road a horseman galloped towards him. In each direction, too, behind these single horsemen I heard the pounding of the feet of a number of horses. Both ways they came, on a run, six or seven riders in each party. At the same moment, in the clear moonlight, they caught sight of Joseph Doane, motionless by the Oak tree, calmly waiting for his two sentries to join him, and such a shouting came up and down the road as I never heard. Two or three pistol shots rang out, and now, I thought, will Joseph Doane certainly be caught and hanged. Still he waited. A moment more, and his sentries gained his side. Now they wheeled their horses abreast with his, all facing the fence on the far side of the road from me. Abreast they took the fence, and side by side crossed the field. Another fence, another field, and they were out of sight, while their pursuers on poorer mounts crowded together at the oak tree, and fired their pistols at objects already out of range.

I had seen enough, and made my way discreetly homewards by the fields to find, when I had reached the house, that the package given me by Joseph Doane contained the exact sum which Moses Doane had taken from me on the way from market. With the money there was a statement in Joseph Doane's careful hand writing, and I suspected that the working of conscience was due more to Joseph than to his brother.

"A Nest of Vipers"

AT THE TIME appointed, leading a second horse, I went to the junction of the city road with the road running to the ford, and after an hour's wait John Spare appeared with the men who had effected his delivery from the gaol. The charge on which he had been taken into custody still hung over him, but it was not likely that he would be brought to trial unless some one of the Doanes were captured, tried and found guilty; and recalling the agility of Joseph Doane, which I had witnessed with the aid of the moon, there seemed no immediate cause for anxiety. John Spare assured his sister and daughter, who seemed to think that he must bear upon his person the marks of prison chains, and were surprised to see him look no different, that he had suffered no particular discomfort, physically, and had preserved a serene mind by recalling how many better men than he—among them John Bunyan and William Penn–had been thrown into gaol.

On the next Saturday he said that we should all go to church as usual in the morning. He contended that what the congregation might be, or the clergyman, or the choir, was of small consequence; that a Christian went to church to worship God, and to render this worship himself, not to have some other person, or persons, worship for him. Mercy Spare said flatly that she would not set foot in such a nest of vipers, but her brother, his daughter and I went as if nothing had happened. Our appearance, especially that of the chief person among us, caused a turning of heads, and whispers of surprise, as we walked up the aisle to the family pew. All knew that John Spare had gone to gaol. Few knew that he was out again, and some of the faces bore an expression showing the sorrow beneath at seeing him at large. After the service I went to the choir loft to recover some articles which Eunice had left there by reason of forgetfulness, and David Wilkinson detained me in talk.

Adam Supplee, the sour-visaged vestryman, was one of the few who had known of John Spare's release, and David portrayed him as being outraged at the failure of justice. Adam had been early at the church door to discuss the laxity of the law with different groups of men. He was convinced that John Spare had been guilty of consorting with the Doanes, and how much more he was guilty of the future would show. Convinced himself, he had set about convincing others, with all the persistence of a narrow nature, which does not understand clearly what it is at, and he had been so successful that some of the congregation began to think of the danger to their homes from John Spare's presence in the neighborhood again. Theodore Morris, David said, had heard some of the harangue, and had declared in no smothered voice that Adam was a fool. While a few were disposed to defend John Spare, at least until he was proven guilty, the mischief had been done with many. When I came out of the church door, Eunice and her father were standing almost alone, many of their former friends having hastened off homeward.

Next, we found that some of the gossip, as well as the fact of John Spare's arrest, had become known in the city market, and we had the mortification of seeing our regular customers standing before other stalls, making their purchases. It was a relief to us when the widow Stevens, who lived on Fourth street, near Pine, came bustling up to our stall, and exclaimed in a loud voice, so that many heard:

"I don't care what they say. I can't get along without Eunice Spare's butter. It is the sweetest and best butter in the market, and everybody knows it, and I don't believe the gossip anyhow. Our people have lost their wits. They would believe that I, myself, am a witch, if someone would start the tale."

John Spare thanked her, and assured her that all would be

set right in due time. However, the widow's sympathy did not sell our farm products, and we had to peddle our things from house to house, though not liking it. After that we did not go to market at all for a time. Then two of the farm hands, through loyalty to the colonies, and for the upholding of public virtue, fell away from us, just as we were beginning to plough for wheat, but Giles and Guilbert and Long Thomas, who remained faithful, denounced the others as renegades, and warned them that they must keep a civil tongue in their heads or stay housed for safety. Mercy and Eunice Spare felt enheartened by this, when it was reported to them, and sent to the field some methleglin to drink. By the time we were ready to dig the potatoes, we heard that a Spare party was growing up in the church, and I began to have hopes that it might yet come right.

Theodore Morris had been on our side from the first, and I was ready to forgive his lofty ways for it. But the rallying point, around which gathered the party in our favour, was the natural opposition to the zealousness shown by Adam Supplee against us. He had been running in the one track, and was wearing it so deep that he could not see over. At first it looked as if he would carry all before him. Then, one by one, men began to reconsider, and to remember his past quarrels with them, and he had quarreled with many—about a steeple on the church, about a new altar rail, about the grave-yard wall, about this and that matter, finding fault, putting obstacles in the way, never able to work with other men, but always in opposition. A number were weary of his ways and of him.

He hailed Abel Strong, so Abel told us, to enforce his view upon him, and held him for half an hour, though Abel was in a hurry to go by. Being now in his favourite line, Adam was working hard, and he had a new thought to broach, one which was so far entirely his own, but for the good of the church and the people, he was ready to impart it to Abel.

“I see you're in a hurry, Abel. I'm a busy man, too, but there are times when private concerns must wait on the public good.”

"Yes, we've all got something to do," Abel answered. "Some in one way; some in another, some with hands, some with tongues."

"Very true, Abel. Very true. Nevertheless, we must find time to circumvent Satan and his plans, or we will be punished for sloth. It's our duty, Abel, and the duty of the church. As church members we can't let this affair of John Spare's go on the way it is going, and not lift a hand to prevent. If you or me was taken up for consorting with highwaymen, would we put on a bold face, and walk up the church aisle as if nothing had happened? You couldn't Abel; no more could I."

"Speaking of highwaymen, and consorting with them," said Abel, "I consorted with them myself. I walked right into John Spare's barn, where they were, and exchanged words with them, and they laid me out in the calf pen. Shan't I walk up the church aisle as if nothing had happened?"

"That was different, Abel."

"How do I know that, Adam? May be John Spare's consorting, as you call it, was like mine, and couldn't be helped, and came about with no wish of his."

"No! No! Abel, wouldn't he have told us so long ago? Has he said a word? No, not one. No, he went to gaol instead. He's acted like a guilty man, Abel, and should be put out of the church. There's others that think so besides me. It will be done. See that you are on the right side, Abel," and Adam Supplee let him go. We had nursed Abel Strong back to health when we thought the horse thieves had done for him, and if the Angel of the Lord ever were to read from his Book, wherein is written the offences of men, anything to question the right of a member of the Spare household to enter the gates of Paradise, Abel Strong, if he were by, would be ready to enter a defence. He repeated to us what Supplee had said to him, and told others of the zealot's plan; and not liking Adam any too well, and remembering his past contrariness, they declared that he was going altogether too fast and too far, and they would knock a spoke out of his wheel. So two parties grew up in the church, and what Adam Supplee's party lost in numbers, more from dislike of Adam than from any conviction of John Spare's innocence, the Spare party gained. Not but what the accused man had staunch friends, who ridiculed the stories about him, as Theodore Morris, to his credit, had done from the start. There were some of these from the very beginning of the trouble. But they were mostly people of more substance than the others, and were in the minority, and dismissing the gossip as of small importance themselves they at first failed to grasp how rapidly a plant of that kind will grow in the fertile soil of narrow minds. It was to these last that Adam Supplee made successful appeal, and among them gained a following in favor of having John Spare withdraw from the church.

"I told you," said Mercy Spare, "they were a nest of vipers."

We got the potatoes out of the ground and stored with the help of Giles, Gilbert and Long Thomas, and wondered what we would do with the crop, being out of favor at the city market as well as at home, and not liking the peddling business. We made all snug for winter again, and were driven in upon ourselves for company and consolation. Fifty cords of wood we burned between October and April in that long cold period.

❧ 16 ❧

Learning the Dutch Roll

THAT WINTER Eunice Spare and I went in the sleigh to no choir practising. We took no part at the Christmas season in adorning the church, and on Christmas Day I thought it had been poorly done for want of Eunice's directing. All David Wilkinson's activity could not put the proper spirit in the Christmas morning music, when Eunice was not in the choir to respond to his understanding of it. The attendance in the pews showed a steady falling off from Sunday to Sunday, for as the winter wore on, the feeling ran high between the parties, who had almost lost sight of John Spare and the charges against him, in the growing wrath at what the contestants were saying against each other. The Rector was at his wit's end to know how to allay the storm, and could only hope it would blow over. Instead of greetings at the church door, and gatherings for friendly talk and exchange of news, there were two camps almost as hostile to one another as the camps of the British and the Americans, and in each group talk was confined to discussion of what the enemy had said or done, and to plans for outwitting the other side. Most of this went over the heads of the Spares, the ones who might be thought the most concerned, like a gale heard among the trees on top of the Stone mountain by a man standing to leeward in the shelter of the base.

The few signs in the Spare household of the storm were mostly given by Mercy Spare when something would move her to speak of "the nest of vipers," or "that Rattlesnake, Adam Supplee." The calmness of John Spare in this time of trial, and loss of repute and money, I have never seen exceeded. We had all been convinced that Eunice was right, and that he was waiting for the proper time to come when he could speak out.

In January the mill dam was covered with ice a foot thick, with a surface like glass, and Theodore Morris brought over his skates to teach Eunice the Dutch roll, which he had learned from Hendrick Van der Sluys, whose grandfather had come from Holland, and they urged me to go with them, Eunice bringing down from the attic for me a pair of skates which had belonged to her father. I had never tried to skate before, the winters in our part of England being too soft to make much ice, and I was but an awkward figure at the sport. But Eunice could soon balance from one outside edge of the skate to the other, almost as well as Theodore Morris could do, and she conceived a passion for the graceful, swaying motion, and afterwards would have me go as often as we could to the ice. After a time, I began to make progress, and did pretty well, and we scarcely missed the choir practice while the skating lasted, and were in danger of forgetting our troubles.

When I walked back to the house with Eunice after two hours on the ice, and saw her cheeks aglow, and her eyes sparkling from the exercise and the sharp air, I was indeed in danger of forgetting John Spare's trouble, and that the present was not a fitting time to bother him with a sweet trouble of my own. Often, when Eunice was not by, I would consider how he would look upon my love for his daughter if I avowed it to her and to him. Without intending it, I had brought safety from the Doanes for him and his by rescuing Joey Doane, and that might have been in my favor, but our good standing with the Doanes was the cause of his going to gaol, and of the disfavor of Adam Supplee and his followers. Still, I thought, he would not blame me for that. Drawn in contrary ways by Eunice's gentleness and capability and good sense and beauty on the one side, and by the trouble we were in on the other, I was in doubt, almost deciding that the time to speak would be when the clouds now hanging over us had cleared away, when I learned something of importance from Mercy Spare. What she knew she had to speak out if there was any body to speak to, and because of this lack of self control, more than once I had thought it just as well that she had given up going to church while there was so much bad feeling there.

A week after Theodore Morris had come to teach Eunice the Dutch Roll, I carried in a back-log for the livingroom fire. Mercy Spare sat there alone, knitting a stocking for one of the boys. She began by complaining that the wood was green. Now we used some green wood to hold the fire, and more seasoned wood for the heat. I was a little out of breath with the weight of the log, and it was not every man who could have carried it alone. Before I had time to remind her of what she well knew, she went on a little petulantly:

"I don't see what is to become of us. One time it's the Doanes; next it's the church people. John goes about as if he had a clamp on his lips. And now Eunice has gone and refused Theodore Morris's offer of marriage, and such a good match! Where will she find such another, or any other for that matter, and she going on twenty-three?"

I had never heard Mercy Spare speak in a way to give me so much pleasure, though her tone of voice might have been improved. Much as I should have liked to hear more, or even the same news repeated, it was something that I could not encourage her to dilate upon, and as best I could, I passed it off as if it were none of my business but a family matter, and went out to my work, thinking that Eunice would not care to have her aunt discuss her affairs in this open way. I felt sure, too, that her aunt was in needless fear lest her niece should have no further opportunity of marriage, now that Theodore Morris was gone.

The next evening there was a full moon, a sky without a cloud, and an air almost without motion. Looking from the window on the lit expanse of rolling fields and hills and woods, Eunice said,

"Richard, let us go, and skate by moonlight."

I joined her at the window, where we could see plainly the bare trees along the stream, but not the stream itself. I was willing enough to go, but her Aunt Mercy objected.

"Eunice Spare," she said, "I should think you could get enough skating in the day time."

"O! you come, too, Aunt Mercy. We'll take the sled, and Richard and I will give you a ride on the ice. Since you stopped going to church, you are in the house all the time. Do come!"

Her aunt refused, and we went off without her, across the meadow, where the long, brown grass was stiff with frost, crushing the white ice formed of what had been shallow pools beneath our feet, to the margin of the frozen stream, where in a few minutes we made a pile of fagots and larger wood, and I started a fire with my flint and steel and a little tinder. We had been skating perhaps ten minutes, and the fire on the bank was blazing high, when we saw another skater coming down the stream towards us. We watched with admiration the ease, confidence and grace of the sweeping curves which brought him to our side, his skill exceeding anything we had ever seen. He said that he had been attracted by our fire, and that he was Hendrick Van der Sluys.

"O!," said Eunice, "then we are just learning the Dutch roll at second hand from you. Theodore Morris taught us," and she gave him our names, Van der Sluys replied pleasantly:

"And third hand from my father, who taught me, and fourth hand from his father who taught him, and brought his skill from Holland."

He told us he had skated down the stream some five or six miles, being tempted on and on, until he had seen our fire and sought company. He was a man of thirty years, of pleasing speech and companionable, and in our present situation it was a relief to foregather with a new acquaintance on something not related to our troubles. After a little urging, and a becoming reluctance on his part to boast, he made known to us several pretty figures to be done on skates, and was patient in instructing us. More than an hour he spent with us in this way to the delight of both of us. Then Eunice invited him to walk to the house and drink some cider.

John Spare, it turned out, knew of Hendrick Van der Sluys and welcomed him with simple hospitality. While Mercy Spare and Eunice fetched the cider, mugs and cake, I learned that our guest had been out in the war as Captain of a militia company, that his home was thirty miles to the westward beyond Falkner's Swamp, and that he was a surveyor engaged for a time in gathering evidence concerning a disputed boundary to an estate, and would be called upon to testify when the case came before the court. We were all pleased with our guest's competent speech and promptness in little things, as if his forebears had brought from the old world, and passed along, graces that were not too common among our people, and which by some were despised. When John Spare told him that I was a surveyor, he expressed interest, and in reply to his questions I told him that owing to the times, I had done little work of the kind in America, and had had leisure lately to study Rittenhouse's new method, which he knew about. After an hour, which was made more agreeable to us by reason of contrast with our loss of friends, he took his departure, promising to return if the ice held good on Saturday afternoon, when we would try the figure skating by daylight.

In the interval, Eunice watched the skies every morning for signs of snow or a thaw, which would spoil the ice, but the weather remained clear and cold, and on Saturday after dinner Van de Sluys reappeared according to promise. Mercy Spare consented to go out on the sled, a while, and the two boys gave us uneasiness by venturing too near the dam breast, until Eunice had to threaten them. Van der Sluys praised her attempts to imitate the feats which he could do with such ease. Nor was his praise mere flattery, for she attempted the untried feats with a confidence and firmness that I could not equal. We made amazing progress in our acquaintance with our new friend, the two boys outrunning their elders in this direction. They were delighted when he accepted Mercy Spare's invitation, seconded by Eunice, to eat supper with us, and for a while after the meal he entertained us with stories of the war and the Indians, among whom he had journeyed to the northward.

When the boys had gone to bed reluctantly, returning two or three times for another word, and we had lit our pipes, Van der Sluys saying that a Dutchman by descent, such as he was, ate only in order to lay a foundation for a smoke, he turned to me and asked if I was a good marksman with the rifle.

"Only fair," I answered.

"O! Captain," Eunice exclaimed, "he's too modest, by half. Richard had never shot with a rifle before coming to America. Now, he picks off the chicken hawks for me, and never misses."

"Then he is more than a fair shot," and turning to me, he continued:

"I have been engaged to survey wild lands far to the North when the spring opens. How would it suit you to go with me, and help with the work. It will take a week on horse-back to reach the lands. I suppose a month to finish the work. In six weeks we ought to be back. The horses will find plenty of grass. We shall have to depend on the rifle mainly for food. Near streams or lakes we can vary the diet with fish. If we have luck, now and then, we may get corn from the Indians. Salt we will carry, and use it sparingly."

My heart leaped when I comprehended this unlooked for prospect, but, almost as quickly, I thought how will it be possible to leave John Spare when he is already short of help.

"How fine," cried Eunice. "Can't I go, too, Captain? Think of it! Day after day, in the great woods! Startled deer drinking by a mirror lake! Grouse springing their drums from behind a tree, and off before you can see them! Night after night under the still skies! Indians stealing along! O! How delightful!"

We all laughed at her enthusiasm, except her Aunt Mercy, who said:

"Yes, rain day after day! Wet clothing! Food running short! And, may be, the Indians on the war path! All very fine to have somebody else boast about it afterwards!"

John Spare now spoke up.

"Richard, if you start with the first grass, you will be back before hay harvest, I can manage to get along until then. It is too good a chance for you to throw it away."

So it was decided that I would give an answer at a later time, and Van der Sluys took his departure.

"Yes, Richard, you should go," said John Spare again. "To

.vork with Captain Van der Sluys will give you standing with others."

❧ 17 ❧

A Secret Made Known

IT WAS still a long time before the first grass. Before Van der Sluys had left our neighborhood, I promised to be ready to go with him to the wild lands, and he said that he was pleased that I could go. He would ascertain the best trails to follow, and as for preparations they would not be many. He would provide a pack horse besides the one he would ride, and I should need only a good horse, a good rifle, powder and balls, and a few articles, which would go on the pack horse. In the meantime, that is before we got away on our journey, several things happened at home.

If I were going away on a long journey into the uninhabited country out of sight of Eunice Spare for six whole weeks, and she had refused to marry Theodore Morris, and I was to have a promising opening as a surveyor, I thought I might tell her what had been in my mind now for many months, but which I had refrained for good reasons from mentioning. So one day, towards the beginning of Spring, I said to her that I had a secret to tell her.

"What, Richard! You have a secret, too? But you know what it is. You are better off than I. I have a secret, but I don't know what it is, though father knows it, and I suspect Judge Morris. Whether Moses Doane knows it, I can't tell."

"Yes, Eunice, I have a great secret, of vast consequences, and you could never guess it in the world."

"Is your secret all your own, or do other persons know it, as my secret is known?"

"In truth, Eunice, I have two secrets which nobody knows

but myself, but one of them I can't tell about." Suddenly having thought of my missing chest with all my money in it, it seemed, when I had said this, that I was growing in shrewdness.

"You have two secrets! You can tell me one of them. The other you must keep. I dislike secrets. I think one secret is enough for anybody, and two secrets, too many for Richard Holt."

"My secret, Eunice, is that I love you. I have loved you for a long time."

I felt within me the stirrings of eloquence, and could have gone on for some time, had I not been surprised by the merriest peal of laughter from her who was my auditor.

"Richard Holt! Richard Holt!" she cried. "Now you must tell me your real secret?"

"Tell you my real secret?" I repeated, amazed.

"Yes, Richard dear," she said putting her hand in mine. "Didn't you promise to tell me a secret which nobody knew but you. Have you fulfilled your promise, Richard? I think—I think not yet, Richard. Never mind. You need not tell me, I know enough to satisfy one maid." So my great secret was out, and it was no secret at all, and I began to have misgivings, and to wonder if her aunt Mercy and her father also knew my secret. No, if her aunt Mercy had known, even she would not have been likely to tell me that Eunice had refused Theodore Morris, and I was consoled with the thought that only so discerning a person as Eunice could have thus read my heart.

Eunice had one condition to make which was that I must speak to her father at once. She could not even give me her promise until her father consented.

"Richard, I am all that father has, and he is in sore trouble," and her eyes filled with tears, even while her lips smiled. So I went to John Spare and repeated my great secret to him. Nor did he seem as much surprised as I thought he would be. But, like his daughter, he gave a qualified consent to my suit.

"Richard," he said, "I have trusted you and you have been worthy. I could trust my daughter with you. But wait awhile. Let things go on as they are. I do not say this to remind you of the want of property. In this country the want of wealth need be no bar to advancement. But when a man asks a father for his daughter's hand, it is right that there should be shown a prospect of advancement. Wait a little until the skies clear, and you see a way opening ahead of you."

In all my time with him, John Spare had never said or done aught to remind me that I was not his equal. But now I saw clearly the need for progress; and though I had a regretful thought for my lost money, I did not feel discouraged when I considered how one could rise in America by making the best of opportunity. Calling Eunice, her father repeated what he had said to me, and taking my hand again in hers she said to him:

"Richard said he had two secrets. One of them he shared with me, and now we have shared it with you. The other secret he keeps to himself. And father, I suspect you of keeping a secret. I told Richard I did not want to know his other secret, and I do not want to know yours, if you have one, until you are ready to tell me; I can wait to hear it, and Richard and I will wait until you are ready to give us your blessing."

Thus it was arranged all very smoothly for so weighty a question, and we went about our work in good heart.

At the approach of Spring, when Easter was near, we learned that at the church the contest between the Spare and the Supplee parties had taken a new direction. The question now was not whether John Spare should go out, but whether Adam Supplee should be put in, whether he should be made a vestryman again. Abel Strong told us that every man in the church was taken by the coat and held fast that he might listen to argument. It was the season of the spring vendues, and David Wilkinson's business as an auctioneer was sadly interfered with, because when a Supplee follower and a Supplee opponent started a debate, as they were sure to do almost as soon as they met, immediately a group of men gathered about them, one after another joining in the argument over the church quarrel. Memories were ransacked, and Adam's whole career was brought to light, and matters uncovered which had been lost sight of. The wives were taking a hand, too, and instead of exchanging the latest news about their babies when they met, were passing one another with great coolness, if they happened to be on opposite sides of the vestry contest. It wasn't much talked of, as being a stream not to be crossed just yet, but nearly every body knew it to be likely that John Spare might go out of the church if Adam Supplee had followers enough to go into the vestry.

Old Jacob Moores, a widower whose daughter, herself a childless widow, kept house for him, was dead and buried. The widowed daughter was going away to live with a married sister. The household goods, the stock, and the crops were all to be sold at a vendue that spring; and later the farm, which was in good order and fertile, would be sold privately if a purchaser could be found, which was doubtful owing to the low state of trade, and the scarcity of hard money. There was plenty of paper money, but people preferred to keep what they had rather than part with their goods and lands for the printed bills. The vendue of old Jacob's possessions was likely to draw many persons to it.

The farm, as we farmers say, was "well watered." There were as many as fifty acres of good timber on it, and it was rich, red-shale land, a little in need of lime, and would grow fine crops of grass and wheat and corn. I had often cast an eye over the place, pleased with the look of it, the buildings snugly nestled together, sheltered from the cold winds of winter and near the spring. Since the revealing of that secret to Eunice which had been no secret, I had begun to let my thoughts dwell upon old Jacob's farm and to wonder who its new owner would be.

There, Jacob Moores had brought his bride and they had reared their children. There, his daughters had been married, and thence they had gone to make homes of their own. Then the aging man and wife had lived alone with their help. Then she had died, and now old Jacob had at last been gathered to his fathers, and the home which for more than sixty years had been his was to be broken up. Would Eunice and I, I thought, go together through this experience called life, until we too should come to the parting, when one would go and the other be left. I thought with envy of the purchaser of the farm. He would be as young as I, perhaps, and take there a bride and rear his children, and live to a sunny old age until that parting which must come to them in their turn—that parting which to the young and strong seems so distant.

With neither purpose, nor money to buy, I went to Jacob Moore's vendue to feast my eyes on what might be mine if my chest had not been lost beyond all hope of recovery. Several of the fields were well set in grass, and the wheat was strong and green, so that the rolling landscape did not have that forlorn look which lately tilled land has when the snow is first gone; and with the fair prospect before me, more than before, I was cast down because means and opportunity had no meeting place. At the house were many women waiting for a chance to make good bargains, or to gain possession of some coveted article of furniture or table ware, and at the barn a crowd of men were already assembled when I arrived, while in the sun a dozen boys were playing the game of corner ball.

Already too, as I soon discovered, a group was discussing our church troubles and I held aloof from it. Among them I saw William Barnes, Francis Unger, George Heacock, Samuel Pearson, Job Tully and Abel Strong. At first they were talking quietly, but soon I recognized Job Tully's voice, blustering as usual, and raised higher and higher in anger. William Barnes, who was given to mocking and jesting, seemed to be teasing Tully, which was something Job could not parry, or put up with long. Job had made known to me long before at the mill that he was not friendly to John Spare. Now John Spare had dropped out of sight in the development of the neighborhood quarrel, and Job was engaged in asserting the virtues of Adam Supplee. I had not heard what Barnes had said to Job, but the men about them had laughed loudly. William Barnes caught a glimpse of me between the heads of the men about him and cried!

"There's Richard Holt. Come over, Richard, and learn what a good man Adam Supplee is!"

I shook my head, but William persisted laughingly, and others called me. William called again:

"Come on, Richard, Adam is getting a certificate of character. Job is going to write it out, and sign it, and carry it around from house to house like a funeral notice."

Now, writing with Job was a thing of labor, and the men laughed again. Thoroughly angry by this time, Job shouted to Barnes,

"Adam's as good a man as you are, and I am, too," and his uncontrolled temper getting the better of him, he rushed at Barnes and struck him with the butt end of a heavy cart whip, which he carried. Barnes fell in a heap, and the frenzied Tully struck at him again and again after he was down. Fair fights growing out of trivial differences were common enough, but Tully's hitting of an unconscious man was against all rules. The groups about the men were surprised into helplessness for the moment, during which I pushed through them, and seizing Tully took his whip from his hand, and held him until he grew quiet. To do him justice, he seemed at last conscious and ashamed of his outbreak, and soon slunk off home, by which time Barnes had come to himself with no bad consequences. Presently, the men told the tale to the women at the house, and there was so much talk and excitement over what had occurred that David Wilkinson was pushed to it to attract and hold the attention of the people, and said afterwards that Tully had spoiled the sale.

The story spread and was amplified in the usual way as it travelled, and it proved the finishing blow to Adam's chances of becoming a vestryman. When the election came off on Easter Monday he received only three votes.

❧ 18 ❧

Moses Doane's Speech

THE SPRING would have to be well advanced with us before Van der Sluys and I could start for the wild lands, where the greater elevations sometimes retained snow and ice, when in our lower country even the corn had been planted. We had arranged to start on a Monday, and I was both impatient and reluctant to go. Eunice helped me mould a sufficient store of rifle bullets, and my saddle horse was freshly shod, and everything made ready for the journey.

On Friday morning, Eunice said,

"We have to-day, and to-morrow, and then you will leave us. We shall all go to church on Sunday. Aunt Mercy, you must go, too. I asked the minister to read next Sunday the Twenty-third Psalm, because Richard is going away for so long a time into the wilderness."

Her aunt said since they had turned Adam Supplee out of the vestry there might be some Christian spirit left among them still, and she consented to go, pleased I thought by the opportunity to return to their church, which she had not attended now for many weeks.

Then I walked towards the barn, and saw riding up the road, a stranger who called me to the road side.

"You are Richard Holt?" he asked.

"Yes."

"I have asked about you, and have been told that you are strong and can be depended upon. I am Jesse Jackson, Deputy Sheriff, I want a posse of six or seven men, and I want you. You know when the law requires you, you have to come. Strong and Pearson and others in the posse recommended that I get you."

I told him that I would go if I must, but was naturally curious to know what I was wanted for.

He threw his leg over the saddle and explained:

"This is for yourself alone. Not a word to anybody. It's only fair a man should know what he is about, I would not have come for you if I had not known you were one to be trusted."

I promised to keep whatever it was to myself, and he suggested that we go to the barn. The road was too public, and he would rather not be seen talking to me. Once within the horse stable he took up his tale, beginning at the beginning and coming down to present times.

"You have heard a good deal no doubt about the disappearance of cattle dealers in these parts?"

I said that many things had surprised me in America, and that was the first surprise, but that I had heard nothing in a long time.

"Well," he said, "we have been on the trail as chance offered ever since. Lately we gained a clue, and we have run it out."

"Where does the trail lead?" I asked.

"Right up to a fellow named Jerry, who was hostler at Bane's tavern. Lately he's been in hiding. He's in a hovel, in the rough country back of Stone Mountain. We take him Saturday night. There is no moon, and if it rains all the better. Bring your gun, and meet me at the cross roads at half past nine. We can reach his hut in less than an hour, and if he has been away in the day, he will be home by that time. If not we'll wait. A dark night will help us. You know Jerry by sight?" he asked.

"Yes, I knew him in England. His name was not Jerry then."

"That's more than I expected. What was he called then?"

"Ferrell. That was his father's name. His mother's, anyhow. Jim Ferrell he was, and he attacked me at night in a Somerset lane, meaning to rob me. I forgave him, and told nobody here but John Spare, hoping he had changed his morals with his name."

"Not he. He's wanted now for something worse than assault and robbery."

There being no choice when the arm of the law lays hold of a man, I promised to be at the cross roads, and the deputy went his way.

On the hour I was at the place appointed. The deputy, Jackson, was already there with Abel Strong, William Barnes, Samuel Pearson, and two or three others, whom I did not know so well. The night was as dark as Jackson could wish, starless, promising rain, but no rain had fallen yet. We had time to spare and rode slowly. All the men knew the object of the expedition, and for the most part we were silent. Jackson had said:

"Men, Jerry is likely to be alone. We shall have no trouble to take him when he knows how many we are. With only two or three, he might show fight. We'll turn off at the lane, tie the horses in the woods, and go to the hut without any noise, on foot. Holt, you and I will take stand at the front. Pearson, you and Heacock guard the rear. Strong and Barnes take the East side of the house, and the others, the west, towards the woods. You all understand? When everybody is at his post I will call on Jerry to surrender. If he resists we shall have to shoot. He's more likely to run. Watch the doors and windows, and you men towards the woods keep a sharp eye on your side. If he runs, that's the way he's likely to hunt shelter."

Little more was said. In another half hour the rain began. We tied the horses in the woods as arranged for, and approached the hut on foot.

"See," said Jackson, as a light showed through the trees, "He's home. We have him."

Two hundred yards from the house, as we were about to separate in order to surround it, Jackson, who was a little in advance, let out a smothered oath, and we heard a voice that belonged to none of our party, in surprised encounter. We crowded forward, as Jackson asked:

"What under Heaven are you doing here, Parsons?"

"I'd like to know, Jackson, what brings you here?"

"What brings me here! I'm after Jerry the hostler."

"Jerry! Why man, you have lost the scent. Jerry isn't here. It's Doane. I'm after him. Keep your voice down."

By this time another party, as large as our own, came out of the darkness, and gathered around Parsons.

"Doane!" said our leader. "I tell you, man, there is no Doane in yonder, it's Jerry."

Parsons seemed taken aback by Jackson's confidence, and Jackson was equally so by Parson's conviction. Each called his followers further away from the house for a conference, and I was mystified to find in Parsons party Theodore Morris and Adam Supplee, the latter pushing his way to the front as was usual with him. When we had withdrawn far enough to speak freely, Adam said in his high, aggressive voice.

"I tell you it's Doane in there. Who would want Jerry. Don't I know? Jerry's on the side of right. Didn't he give me the clue where to find Doane and didn't I tell Parsons? I guess I know all about it. You can't fool me with a cock and bull story about Jerry."

"Who are you," said Jackson.

"I'm Adam Supplee. Everybody around knows who I am, and I know it's Doane in that hut."

"Maybe you know more than I do, but you don't know that Moses Doane is the man who put me after Jerry, and I'd advise you not to claim too much knowledge of the hostler."

"Say, Jackson," said Parsons, as if light were dawning upon him, "did Doane expect you here to-night?"

"No, he didn't. I let him think I should not be ready for a week and would have to be down near Darby to-day."

"Well, Jackson, no more is Jerry looking for me, I didn't confide in him any more than you did in Doane. You've got the papers to take Jerry and I have the papers to take Doane. Maybe they are both in the hut. But what for? What for, after Doane had betrayed Jerry to you, and Jerry had betrayed Doane to me?"

Adam Supplee was too much amazed by the situation to hold the position of prominence which he always sought, and had just attempted, and by this time had dropped into the background. The other men seemed almost as much dumbfounded as he.

"Of course," said Jackson, "each rascal has had his motive for betraying the other. That is for the court to find out, if it cares to know."

I now spoke up saying that I might know something of the motive of Jerry and something of that of Doane, and that when the trial came off I could explain if called on.

"We haven't time to hear about motives, now," Jackson replied. "Parsons is after Doane and I'm after Jerry. We will work together, boys, and if the two are in the hut, take them both."

We had enough men now to encircle the hut. Jackson stole forward and when he returned reported that through the window he had seen both Doane and Jerry seated on stools at a table eating. When all the men had quietly taken their positions, first Jackson called in a loud voice on Jerry to surrender, and Parsons repeated the demand to Doane. At once the light inside was blown out, and I heard the click of cocking rifles start around our circle of men.

Parsons called again:

"Come, Doane, it is no use. Give yourself up, and save trouble!"

"That you, Parsons!" came the voice which I well remembered of Moses Doane, in scoffing answer. "Didn't know you in the dark. You're out late." And then, "Say, Parsons, how many men have you?"

"Fourteen or fifteen. No chance for you, Doane!"

Doane seemed to be considering, and we hoped that he would give himself up. Presently he called:

"Parsons, seeing you have so many men, why don't you make a rush?"

"All in good time, Doane. All in good time. No hurry."

"Well, Parsons, let us have a parley first, and then give me fifteen minutes to think about it."

"If I grant a parley, will you play fair?"

"You can have it all your own way, Parsons. Bring up a half dozen men to the window, and I'll strike a light so you can have a fair mark at Jerry, if he starts to play foul. No shooting until the lights are out, and every man is back in his place."

Parsons and Jackson, with some others, went to the window, and all on that side of the hovel could hear plainly what passed. I could see Doane pretty well, and so many were the man's disguises, that I should not have known him in the semi-darkness, except for his voice.

"Who is it that wants Jerry," he asked.

"I do. Jackson, deputy sheriff."

"Well, Jerry and I can't quite agree. You've got fourteen, or fifteen with you? Yes, I see," as some of the men moved towards the hut. "I'm rather in favor of giving up, but I can't persuade Jerry, and we are on the same side now, we on the inside; you on the outside. Hope you're not getting wet, Jackson!"

"See here, Doane," said Jackson with impatience. "If you have aught to say, say it."

"Don't hurry now, Jackson. Parsons said he was in no hurry."

The rain was falling fast and faster, and we men on the outside were by this time getting a good wetting, standing, as we were, in the open, unsheltered by a single tree, and all of us shared Jackson's impatience.

Parsons now spoke up with, "What is it now, Doane? What is it?" and Adam Supplee, recovering his voice, declared that he had neither seen nor heard Jerry, and he didn't more than half believe he was inside.

"Tell me, Doane," he called, "is Jerry there?"

"Jerry! Jerry!" came the reply, "Jerry who? There's one Jerry here, and Jim Ferrell, and Tom Lumpkins, and Will Thomas, and may be others. All from different parts of the country."

Some of us understood what the grim jester meant, but none of us knew that Jerry had so many aliases, and Adam was quiet again when the drift of Doane's reply was pointed out to him.

"Enough of this, Doane. Tell us what you want to parley about or we go back," said Parsons.

Doane, with the assurance and self confidence that had seen him through many a tight place, leaned out the window, his elbows on the sill, and beginning, with the impudence that was natural to him, said:

"Friends, you honor me by your numbers, and you have spared me trouble; I had intended, on occasion, telling what fools the people hereabouts have been making of themselves, and explaining in a simple way, so they could understand, why all this misbehaviour. Perhaps, I shall never be able to address so many of you in a way so convenient to myself. This is a good roof, I wish I could invite you in. No matter. What I wanted you all to know, and to spread abroad as truthfully as you can, is that some of you made a stupid blunder when you thought that John Spare had any dealings with us Doanes. I learned that John Spare and Judge Morris had something between them, and thought that my knowledge could be made profitable. I told Spare at the Philler vendue what I had discovered, but it was no use; he would do nothing. I thought to frighten him with a threat. Nothing came of it. We Doanes, may be, would have touched up some of his hay crop, to let him know we were in earnest, and some five of us were at his hay stack at dark, when we found there my brother's child, that had floated down the big freshet, and Richard Holt had drawn from the flood, and the Spare women had nursed back to health, and fed and clothed, and kissed, as if he was their own, and none of them knew him from Adam's child. Little Joey Doane talks about them yet, and says the prayer at night which John Spare's women taught him. It is for this that we Doanes told the Spares that they would be safe from us at home and on the road. I learned Jerry here, or Jim, or Tom, or whatever his name is, had played a foul trick on the Spares by telling that John Spare and the Doanes consorted together, and how the neighbors fell away from the Spares, and some of the church people along with that blockhead, Adam Supplee, that Jerry, here, filled full of suspicion, and how, in the city, people would not buy anything from the Spare farm. I knew what Jerry had been doing on his own account, and I took a short cut across the wood-lot to stop his mischief, and to set John Spare right before the world. Jackson can tell you something about Jerry, if he wants to. I knew that Jerry had gone along to keep the dogs quiet on the night the horses were taken from John Spare's barn, and not a Doane had a thing to do with it. That's all, friends. Now, Parsons, give me fifteen minutes to reason with Jerry, and then we'll either surrender or take our chances."

The light went out, and we withdrew to something like our former positions, except that the men interested in Doane's story mingled more together, and talked about what they had heard. The fifteen minutes had nearly gone by when Jackson said to me:

"Jerry must be completely cowed or we should have heard from him after Doane's speech."

Our leaders conferred together as to what to do, whether to make a rush on the hovel, try to set fire to it or wait until morning in case the men did not surrender. Parsons thought it would be better to wait a whole week, and starve the men out, than to attempt any one of the three methods suggested. We could send for food, he said, and take turns at sleeping. I objected, saying that I must be off to the wild lands with Captain Van der Sluys on Monday. The time of respite had fully expired. Parsons had left me, and I was alone when a figure, which I did not remember having seen before, came slowly towards me. It seemed to be that of an elderly man, a little feeble. Coming quite close, a voice said in my ear:

"Holt, I did not think you would be here."

I turned quickly; the figure was gone. The voice was that of Moses Doane. Reluctant as I was to do so, I gave the warning, I shall not say at once, but so quickly that Doane could not have been more than a few feet away. He was gone, and all knew it. No pursuit was possible in that rough and wooded country in the dense darkness. We rushed to the hut, and there on the floor lay Jerry, bound and gagged, as Doane had left him, and scattered about were a wig and some wearing apparel which the highwayman had had no immediate use for. On the whole, if one was to be taken and the other go free, I thought that the better man had escaped.

In the first hours of a new Sabbath we rode away. Before we parted on our different home–leading roads, I had some talk with Theodore Morris, and learned that he had been pressing the hunt for Doane, which explained his night rides in our part of the country that had caused comment. The rain ceased. The stars came out, and a warmer glow in the East heralded the coming dawn as I entered the Spare house, having by this time begun to understand Doane's presence in the hovel with Jerry, and his reason for the declaration from the window. Not expecting the descent upon the place for another week, nor guessing that Parsons would be on a Doane trail at the same hour, he had probably gone to the hut to make sure of Jerry's whereabouts. In some way, from some of Jerry's associates, probably, Adam Supplee had learned of Doane's presence. Adam had fallen now into a deep silence, and we had learned little from him. When Doane found himself surrounded with but a small chance to escape, and had determined not to be captured alive, he had taken what might be the last chance he would ever have to show that the Doanes were not without a sense of gratitude and honour. Even as we rode away from the scene of his escape, the remarks of the members turned to the latest display of cleverness by Moses, but still more to the convincing revelation that he and his family had a share of some of the better traits of humanity.

☙ **19** ❧

The Highlands

"THE SECRETS are all coming out. Soon there will be not one left," said Eunice, when I had told my story to the assembled family before breakfast, and during the meal, and in truth all the way to church, with many repetitions, and many questions asked, and many exclamations of wonder from the women. According to Jackson's injunction, I had revealed nothing before hand of the purpose of my night ride, and the relief and thankfulness for the lifting of suspicion from John Spare were boundless. Mercy Spare always held her head high, but now she rode like a warrior of old erect in a chariot going to triumph over despised foes.

The whole story had preceded us to church, and at the door, led by Pearson, Barnes and Strong, was assembled such a throng as had not been seen there in many Sundays, men and women, all with smiling faces and extended hands to welcome John Spare back to good fellowship, so be it that he would let bygones be bygones. I think that Barnes and Pearson would have raised a cheer if it had not been Sunday, and the minister looking on.

Pleasant is the shelter after storm, spiritual food after longing, and the comfort of human sympathy and understanding when they have been cut off. How Mercy Spare enjoyed her hour of triumph! The people had seen the evil of their ways, and had been brought around again to good behaviour. If she could not forgive them their offences, at least she would ignore what many had said and done, and so she strode into her pew. But as her brother had not been cast down, neither was he now exalted, and very suitably and without effusion he returned the well–meant greetings extended him by some who were straight forwardly apologetic and by others who shamefacedly floundered through their excuses.

I saw Eunice Spare turn to speak to the minister before he went to put on his robes. Then David Wilkinson hurried to Eunice and me, and asked us to sing in the choir. Eunice smiled at me a "Shall we?" and so we did, and I never heard Eunice's voice come fuller and truer or with more feeling, than in the earnest words of the Venite, "O come let us sing unto the Lord; let us heartily rejoice in the strength of our salvation." Then instead of the psalms appointed for the day, the minister read, as Eunice had requested, because I was going on a long journey to the wild country, the twenty-third psalm, beginning, "The Lord is my shepherd; therefore can I lack nothing."

"He shall feed me in a green pasture, and lead me forth beside the waters of comfort."

And

"Yea, though I walk through a valley of the shadow of death, I will fear no evil, for thou art with me, thy rod and thy staff comfort me."

Little thought had I given to any danger on the journey, but Eunice had thought of it, and more than once, when I was far away, and had escaped some passing peril, the solemn words of the psalm and a sweet vision of her who had prompted the minister to say them came to me. Then, just before the final prayers, there fell from the good man's lips the Thanksgiving for restoring public peace at home;

"O Eternal God, our Heavenly Father, who alone makest men to be of one mind in a house, and stillest the outrage of violent and unruly people; we bless thy holy Name, that it hath pleased thee to appease the seditious tumults which have been lately raised up amongst us; most humbly beseeching thee to grant us grace that we may henceforth obediently walk in thy holy commandments; and leading a quiet and peaceable life in all godliness and honesty, may continually offer unto thee our sacrifice of praise and thanksgiving for these thy mercies towards us; through Jesus Christ, our Lord, Amen."

I felt that the prayer must have come from every heart present, as it did from my own, and I wished that Adam Supplee had been at church to hear it. With John Spare's trouble cleared up, and no difficulty about his getting help for the farm work, I was off early the next morning with a light heart to join Captain Van der Sluys.

I have never been able to take that melancholy pleasure in partings which causes many persons to linger over them, to say over and over again what has been said before in a poor attempt to gain a few minutes more of the company of loved ones, to turn back again and again, and to let both voice and face take part in a revel of grief. Nor did Eunice Spare assume any woebegone look when I was ready to start, but cheerily and with courage she saw me go, keeping any misgivings she may have felt within her own breast. For both of us the service at the Church had expressed all that we could feel or hope for. Had either of us known a part of what the summer had in store for me, perhaps, outwardly we should not have kept so calm a demeanor. I knew from the psalm, which she had asked the minister to read, that she had thought of the dangers that lie in wait in the wilderness, and just before I mounted my horse, she had said:

"Richard, I shall pray every day for your safety."

At the first bend of the road I turned, and saw the family group standing at the door each member waving me a farewell. I flourished my hat in the air, and rode out of sight.

Captain Van der Sluys had made all his preparations for our going when I reached his home. The pack of necessary articles, compass and barometer were ready to be placed on the pack horse in the morning. He said that we should go by way of the Delaware valley, although the route was longer, but for a hundred miles at least we should avoid the mountains. Starting early the next morning we made our way to the great river and followed its course to a spot where a mighty volume of waters, ages ago, broke through the mountains with a power, which to think of filled me with awe at the ordering of the elements. Beyond that place we left the river on our right, crossed a range of higher mountains, and went on to near the forty second degree of latitude.

Whereas, the trees were in full leaf about us at the starting point of our journey, in a few days on the higher elevations we had overtaken the Spring, and in this highland forested with great hemlocks, hard maples and beeches, the trees were just putting out their leaves. The barometer indicated that we were nearly 2000 feet above sea level, and the air was keen enough to make our camp fire a comfort. We came upon several lakes and numerous deer drinking from the waters, saw the signs of bears, and heard wild cats in the woods, but had encountered no Indians. It was now the second week of our journey, and the last settlement had been left far behind us. I had not conceived the difficulty of making our way through the mountain forests, where the trees, safe from any four-footed foe, in truth possessed the earth, as yet unattacked by man, the only enemy, except decay and storms descending from the heavens, that could over-turn them. Twice we had passed places where for a mile or more great hemlocks had been laid low by the winds, as if an army of gigantic mowers had swung their scythes through the forests. But with these exceptions the saplings had grown to maturity, and old age, and fallen with decay, and lain where they fell, until resolved again into the mother earth whose breast had nourished them. Their trunks, borne up by the limbs at one end, and the uptorn roots at the other, often posed a barrier to progress as high as a man's shoulders, and compelling us to pick our way, had delayed us, so that what we had expected to accomplish in seven days had taken ten, and I began to think I should not be at home in time for hay harvest. We had made camp in a great elevation at the forest's edge, overlooking a nar-row, winding valley, some ten miles in length. Our horses unused to climbing such long and abrupt heights as they lately had surmounted, and missing their daily measure of grain, although last year's dried grass was abundant, and new grass was well started, were showing signs of fatigue, and we proposed to give them a day's rest before going on. So we erected a shelter hastily, as the wind was in the southern quarter, presaging rain, Captain Van der Sluys said, more surely than an East wind. I asked him for an explanation of this, and he said that the moisture of the warmer air, borne by the South wind against these cooler elevations, was condensed and fell in rain, and that his father had told him that a like process could be seen going on daily in the mountains of the West Indies, where he had once been.

On the ground under our shelter we laid a quantity of hemlock boughs for our beds, and we took time to thatch the inclined roof so that it would turn rain well, and we gathered a good store of dead wood, and put it under cover before we cooked an evening meal of wild fowl, which we had shot. We hobbled the horses in the long grass by a small brook near us, and when we had eaten the birds, lay upon the hemlock boughs in our shelter, and watching the camp fire blaze in front of the open side, which faced away from the rising wind, thought ourselves well prepared for the coming storm.

Now, for a day or two, I had wondered why we had come so far North when the direction of the wild lands which we were to locate, lay as I understood, more to the West. This my leader now explained.

"Richard," he said, "we are now about thirty miles North East of the Susquehanna, and until we have crossed it there will be little more hill climbing to do. I think we are now far enough North to make a crossing with safety."

I thought he spoke of finding a ford or some other place where a crossing could be made with the horses.

"It is not altogether that," he said. "We have come this far North in order to cross the river above the Wyoming settlement, where last year the British, Indians and Tories massacred the old men and boys while the able-bodied men were away fighting with the Americans. I do not know what the present state of things is at Wyoming. The survivors of the massacre were driven out. Whether they have returned, whether the Indians and the New York Tories who settled in the valley and participated in the massacre are still there, I do not know. But whoever is there, it would not be a safe place for us. The Connecticut people who are patriots would not welcome Pennamites, as they call the Pennsylvania claimants. Indians and Tories would make short shrift of a Continental soldier, if they should catch him. That is why we will go in the back way, instead of approaching by the front door, up the valley of the Susquehanna. From here, I think, we may take a course due SouthWest to our destination, leaving the Wyoming country to the Southward."

Rain set in during the night and continued for three days, a hard semi-tropical rain, brought by the South wind, and held us fast in our camp except on the first day, when we were driven forth in search of game, and fortunately came upon some wild turkeys. They were poor in flesh, but served our purpose, and we busied ourselves with cooking and packing enough of the meat to last until we had got well beyond the river, where we should have to exercise caution. The hemlock trees under which we had built, and the thatch on our shelter kept us fairly dry, and we could see the horses caring for themselves with abundant grass and water. All the second night the rain fell in great volume, and in the morning we saw such a sight as I had never beheld before. In the deep valley below us the little creek was swollen to a river. I thought it fortunate that we had not made camp on its banks. The waters coming down the steep hills to this creek had leaped from their courses, and cut out new troughs, as straight as a plough's furrow. On a level with our shelter, and scarce a hundred yards away, was the mouth of a ravine whose banks at the exit were not more than forty feet high, and gradually lessened in height for a distance of three hundred yards to the starting point of the ravine. Before daylight we were awakened by a great roar, and when it was light, saw that the ravine had spewed forth from its mouth a great mass of earth, small stones, rocks and boulders, and one of these boulders, which had been moved by the waters a distance of fifty yards, we judged weighed as much as five tons. We looked about for the horses anxiously, and presently discovered them in a growth of Spruce trees upon higher ground, where they had found safety from the rising streams.

On the fourth day we set out again through the great forest, making but slow progress, though we soon began to descend towards the river valley; and on the next day cautiously approached the river bank, where we were now on the margin of a hostile country. Tethering the horses in the forest, and fastening pieces of sacking with holes at the nostrils, over their noses, so that the sound of any neighing would be smothered, we went out on foot to cast about for signs of Indians or hostile whites, and to search for a crossing place. We went up and down the river for several miles each way, and at last, where there was shallow water for the most part, except for a channel near the opposite shore, came upon the ruins of a burned house, destroyed, as we thought, in the year before. We saw no signs of recent life, and waiting until dusk, crossed the river in safety, the horses having to swim only at the narrow channel.

Once in the shelter of the woods on the western side, we tethered the horses again, ate our cooked food, and lay on the ground to sleep, starting once more as soon as we could see. Though the distance in a straight line was not more than thirty miles, it took us three days more to climb the mountains, and reach our destination on the great table land of the Alleghenies. Here, on the back of the range, was a nearly level space, some ten or twelve miles broad, the height being five or six hundred feet greater than the highest country back of us. On each side of the level land the mountains fell away abruptly, and beyond their deep valleys appeared to roll away, as far as the eye could see, like the billows of an ocean. Here, too, were the hemlocks, and in one direction a region of mighty White Pine trees, while lower down on the mountain sides were the hard woods, Black Cherry trees, with the first branches thirty feet from the ground, and the noble Cucumber tree in great abundance. Covering this table land and the mountain sides for many square miles lay the domain, which we were to locate with as much exactness as possible, and here we should be kept for a month or more. We found that there were two lakes on the mountain top, and by the shore of the larger one we made our camp, this time taking pains in building a snug shelter for ourselves and one for the horses—that for the animals being stout enough to make them secure against wolves. In this inaccessible and rugged region, difficult of approach, we felt safe from the Indians, unless unknown to us we had been seen at the river crossing, or they should come across our trail in the valley.

At Captain Van der Sluy's request I had abandoned my habit of addressing him by his military title, using instead his Christian name, Hendrick. He explained that if we should encounter white men in this enemy's country, and I should address him as Captain, it would excite curiosity and suspicions, and they would want to know which side he was on. In many small ways the need for caution was impressed upon me by my experienced leader, more by example than by precept. Our cooking fire was built in a kind of natural cave, whose overhanging rock distributed the smoke instead of permitting it to ascend in a straight column, and we were careful to use wood which burned freely. We took fish from the lake, set traps for small animals, and used the rifle as little as possible. After we had shot a deer, we found that the meat, in the cool, dry mountain air, kept well, especially when cut into strips and cured.

Six weeks went by, and our work was not quite done, but nearly so. In all this time we had seen neither Whites, other than ourselves, nor Indians. Nor from the forest had there come to us any sounds save the call of birds, the crash of some falling monarch of the woods, now grown senile and tumbling to decay, the splash of a fish in the lake, the laps of the waters on the quiet shores, or the roar of the falls on the lake's outlet. We had left the exploration of this outlet to the last day. It started near our camp, and now we had worked around the four sides of the great tract of wild land to near the starting point. On the morrow we planned to go down the outlet; but on this day

Van der Sluys slipped on a covered stone and injured his ankle, so I offered to go down stream alone upon the following day. The general direction indicated that the water course was near to being, if not altogether, a natural boundary of that section of the tract. In the evening we talked about the probability of this being the case, and then fell into a general conversation of more freedom than of late had been usual with us. Perhaps, it was the thought of home that set our tongues loose.

"Hendrick," I said, "if men lived in the forest long, they would grow into a silence as deep as its own. Have you noticed how little talking we do?"

"It is always so in the great woods," he replied. "Once I was off alone for three months on work like this, and I felt myself more and more of an Indian each week, and when I returned to the settlements, seemed to have lost the desire and power of light speech. Here we come to speak only when speech is necessary. With many persons about us there is so much talking that the doing of things is impeded."

"And I expect that at home they are talking of us, and wondering why we have not returned. The hay harvest will be over without my help," and thinking of Eunice Spare, I added, "I wish they knew how little danger we have met."

"No," he said, "there was some danger at the river, but we were fortunate. We have had little to endure beyond fatigue and sometimes discomfort. However, we are not out of the woods yet, and will need to be careful as we return."

"Do we go over the same route," I asked.

"No, I think we shall go Southwardly from here, and leave the Wyoming Valley well to the East of us, and strike the Susguehanna well below it. I do not like to try again our luck at crossing the river in a hostile country. Luck might fail us. To be seen by a single Indian fisherman would start a hunt for our scalps."

In the morning, taking my rifle, pocket compass and barometer, besides the book of notes, which contained the record of our six weeks' work, and enough jerked venison for the day,

I started down the lake's outlet alone. The memoranda and the sketches in the note book we copied in another book, which we did not carry about with us when in the woods. So abrupt was the fall of the stream, that I found its descent no easy task. Often only by holding fast to a tree limb with both hands, and letting my body out at full length could I find a slippery footing for my feet. Many times I had to wade the stream from one side to the other to make any progress past the boulders, wet with spray from the numerous water falls, the tangle of Rhododendron bushes and under-growth of shrubs and the sheer wall rising from the water's edge. I was amazed at the number of water falls. As I stood by one wondering at its beauty, several times, two more, one above me and one below, were included within a short turn of the stream, and passing these, I would come upon another fall, and still another, and more beyond. In the pools, trout in great numbers darted from under the rocks or attempted to make their way against the on-rushing waters. Occasionally, I stopped to note in the book a conspicuous landmark or the compass bearings, and when I estimated that I had come a little more than a mile, not more than a mile and a quarter, and had arrived at a comparatively level reach of the water, I found that I had descended one thousand feet, and felt the joy of a discoverer. I thought that I should have a tale to tell Hendrick Van der Sluys and to the Spares when I got home again.

Below the level reach of waters, I came upon a canyon whose walls rose straight from each side of the water, and to make my way down it I had to take to the stream, there being no foot-hold on the sides. By the time I had emerged from this, I judged that I had reached the limit of the tract, and concluded that the stream would do well enough for a boundary, though it might not be in every part precisely upon the line. I saw that night would overtake me before I could make my way back, so I ate and slept where I found myself, and the next day, with even greater labor than on the previous day, climbed, crawled and dragged myself, up past the pools, with their fishes, and the tumbling water falls, one after another, advancing with such slowness that the day was nearly spent when I reached the mountain top.

I expected to see Hendrick Van der Sluys on the watch for me, and was well nigh to bursting with eagerness to describe to him the wonders of the mountain stream. I had no skill in language to convey to him a realization of its beauty, but I knew that if I told him, or any surveyor for that matter, that the waters ran down hill at the rate of a thousand feet within a mile and a quarter of their length, it would be understood. Even now, many years after the happenings, which I am writing down for my brother, Robert, in England to read, the measurement of the great plunge made by that stream down the mountain side brings back to my mind a clearer image of its wonders than any form of description could do. I have noticed that the great poet, Shakespeare, whose writings printed in the city in the year 1795 I have, when he sings of the many glorious mornings he had seen, attempts not to describe every detail of the approach of day, but sets forth a feeling, which the reader in a right condition of mind can feel too.

At last I was at the summit, and somewhat eagerly made my way through the border of the forest until I came into the open, where our shelter and stable had stood. Nothing remained of them but piles of ashes and charred logs, which were still smouldering. Of Hendrick Van der Sluys, the horses, the articles that were in the cabin, there was not a sign.

❧ 20 ❧

A Misadventure

MORE THAN ONCE in my life I have been ashamed of unworthy thoughts that have come to me in moments of surprise, and have hoped that in reality they were not thoughts, but an outbreak of instincts released from their leash. Suddenly, now, there came upon me the fear that I had been abandoned, and I thanked God that the fear went as soon as it came, and with it the ugly suspicion that I felt like doing penance for. In the place of this momentary weakness, there followed a clearer conviction that in my absence Van der Sluys had been attacked, and either killed or captured by the Indians. The burning of our cabin I could account for in no other way.

In my excitement and dismay I forgot my fatigue. I still had a little dried venison in my pouch. I had my rifle, a moderate quantity of powder and balls, the record of our work and the pocket compass and barometer. For that matter, I should have felt no uneasiness about finding my way without the compass, unless under a constantly clouded sky. All signs of direction other than the compass, the sun and the stars I had seen fail too often to place dependence in them. I have known the best woodsmen to be lost under a clouded sky, and had seen the moss to grow on all sides of too many trees to regard it as of much value as a guide then or afterwards. Nor did the loss of the horses discourage me. Until the settlements were reached, I could make better time on foot than when impeded in the difficult forests by the horses. The nearness of a foe increased the danger of obtaining a supply of meat, and then I thought of the traps, and hoped to find something in them. With food, and undeterred by white or the Red men, I could reach home on foot in nine or ten days. I considered whether it was possible for me to find out if Van der Sluys were dead, or if not, whether I could rescue him, and thought that unless I came upon his body by accident, there was small chance of my learning his fate, and if he were alive, there was less chance of my effecting his rescue. Nevertheless, I set about doing what could be done while the light lasted. We had pulled off from the horses' feet their shoes, overgrown by the hoofs, several weeks before, and therefore, except in damp places, I did not expect to follow their trail readily; but after searching for a long time, I found on the far shore of the lake, where the hoof prints led into the forest. It was now dusk, and I could go no further until morning.

With the approach of night, the degree of confidence which had come back to me ebbed away again. The Whip-poor-Wills had begun to set up their mournful cry. The forest took on a loneliness, unfelt as long as I had human company. I found myself trying to avoid stepping upon the dry sticks scattered on the forest floor, and in other ways striving to move about silently. I tried to shake off this nervousness without much success and to spur myself into a more confident condition of body, but in spite of all efforts, my eyes sought the ground in the instinctive attempt to move about without making a noise. Raising my eyes from the ground, I was astonished and overjoyed to see Van der Sluys standing on the edge of the forest by the lower end of the lake. He had seen me but had not called, and now when I looked up, by signals gave me to understand that I was to go through the edge of the woods towards him, and each covering about half of the distance we soon met.

I told him of my fear that he had been killed or captured by the Indians, and of my relief and joy at seeing him alive and free. Mortally weary, now, after the two days' climb up and down the lake's outlet, and the stimulus of the fresh excitement having lost its effect, I lay upon the ground while Hendrick told me of his adventures of the two days. Tiring of inactivity, after my early departure, and finding his ankle better, he had hobbled the horses in luxuriant grass at some distance away, taken his rifle and surveyor's compass, and walked a couple of miles across the woods to repeat some observations, which he had wished to confirm. At noon he returned, and as he approached the opening about the lake, saw disappearing into the forest and headed towards the South West four men, whether Indians or Whites, at that distance, he could not tell, and our cabin and stable burning with a fire that had been but lately started. Whether the disappearing incendiaries belonged to a larger party, or whether they were still in the vicinity, or whether with their plunder they were returning to the Wyoming country, he did not know. Expecting my earlier return, he had kept a constant watch for me during the morning of the second day, and then driven by the need of food had gone off to inspect our traps, and was returning with a couple of hares when he saw me. He had not thought it prudent to approach the site of the cabin by daylight on the day before, but after dark he had gone to a receptacle among the rocks, at some distance from the cabin, to search for our emergency store of powder and rifle balls. We had concealed the ammunition wrapped in several pig-bladders and skins, and this store the marauders had not discovered. Some of the powder was damp, he said, but in the morning, if the sun shone we could dry it. I still had left some of the jerked venison of which we ate; and then stretching myself on the ground, I lost our trouble in the deep slumber of which I was so much in need, while Henry went to bring the horses back to water. Seven hours I slept, awakening with a feeling that the night had fled in the time of a brief nap. For some reason my sleepless night on the potato bags on the floor of The Bell tavern came back to me, and I wondered why a man in safety should be wakeful, though weary, and with danger surrounding him should sleep like a babe. Van der Sluys was already preparing the hares, and although there was some risk in it, we made a fire by our overhanging rock, cooked them, and ate. We had spread the powder out thin where the first sun's rays should fall upon it, and as soon as it was dried somewhat, set off on a course due South.

The incendiaries had made a South westwardly start. The Wyoming settlements lay to the East of us. We hoped the way South was open and pressed forward with all possible speed, halting only at noon to expose our store of powder to the sun again, to eat of our cooked game and berries of various kinds which grew in great abundance, and to give the horses an hour's browse in the grass. The descent from the mountain top on the Southern side was even more difficult than the ascent of it had been. When the sun showed it to be about four o'clock, we came upon a valley crossing our course from the westward, and falling away to the distant river valley. In an hour more we had reached the stream flowing through it, and stopping only long enough for the horses to drink, urged them onward with the object of covering as much distance as possible while daylight held. We had gone not a hundred yards when four white men with rifles drawn stepped out of the shrubbery. One of whom commanded us to dismount and come forward without our guns. They were clad in the garb of the woods, and at a distance it would have been hard to tell whether they were whites or Indians. Van der Sluys whispered to me that he thought them the men who had set fire to our hut. The leader, a lithe, powerfully built man of my own age, asked,

"Who are you, and what is your business here?"

Hendrick replied that we were honest men, surveyors employed to locate wild lands.

"I know you are surveyors. I have your book. But do you call yourselves honest men, squatting on land with no rightful warrant, and taking a tract which belongs to Connecticut."

"I know nothing about rival claims," Hendrick readily answered. "Our surveying has been done, not for ourselves, but for them that employed us. If you have cause for quarrel it is with them, not with us."

"We will teach the Pennamites not to send their agents into this country. Your work shall go for naught, and your book shall go with you to Connecticut."

The speech of this man, the use of his voice, the manner of pronouncing his words was different from anything I had ever heard, either in England or America, and always depending upon the sound of the voice as a guide to the user's habit, I did not relish the prospect of his company any more than I liked the idea of a journey of 200 miles to Connecticut, a journey which, if made in the right direction, would more than carry us home, although it mattered little, since our captors were double our numbers and possessed our fire arms as well as their own. Hendrick now asked the man by what authority he took it upon himself to interrupt two peaceful men and honest, who as far as we knew had acted within our rights.

"By authority of the law of Connecticut," came the answer. "But no matter what the authority is, you go with us."

By direction of the leader, whom his companions called Adams, two of the men drew the charges and gave us our useless rifles to carry, and preceded by two of the party and followed by the other two, we led our horses back to the stream which we had crossed but a little while before and there camped for the night. The Connecticut men shared their food with us, and required us to carry wood for the fire, but did not trust us with the axe, and we were compelled to care for the horses under the eyes of a guard with a loaded rifle.

In a rude way our captors were not uncompanionable after a day or two. Every night two of them made a long prayer, the longest I ever heard, and I wondered why the prayer failed to soften their conversation by day, which was at times uncouth and boorish. Taking my cue from Hendrick, who was wise beyond many, we fell more or less into the ways of the men, and I could see that gradually they were beginning to treat us with a kind of ill-mannered respect. They were surprised by the knowledge which Van der Sluys casually showed of the stars and the constellations, when they rose, where they were in the heavens at different hours of the night, and when they set, so that at any hour of a cloudless night he could tell the time and points of the compass. Adams, the leader, and another had eager though untaught minds, and after a while they were asking both Hendrick and me questions about this and that, both in America and England; and seated about the camp fire when the day's journey was done, they would talk with great volubility and confidence about matters of which they knew nothing. They were not expert marksmen with the rifle, and wasting a good deal of ammunition had to draw upon our store, and we began to fear that they would soon shoot that away in the air. One day when they had missed several grouse by lack of quickness, Hendrick said,

"Let me try, the next time."

To my surprise Adams consented, and when Hendrick brought down the grouse, would have him try again, and then Hendrick missed, which also surprised me, for he was a rare marksman with the rifle. Then Hendrick told me to shoot, and I was luckier than Van der Sluys had been, getting two of the birds. After that, they let us carry our rifles loaded, and I thought them losing their wariness. All the while we were going further and further from home, with no chance yet of severing quietly our forced companionship and permitting our captors to go on their own way, unburdened with our care, unless we had been ready to do murder, and that we could not do. Steadily we had made progress towards a better acquaintance, especially after the third night, when seated around our camp fire, Van der Sluys and I sang together several Dutch songs, "William of Orange" and "Bergen op Zoom," which Hendrick's grandfather had brought from Holland, and Hendrick had taught me, followed by some rousing English songs of Cromwell's time, which I had taught to him. On the fourth day of our captivity, after dark, I heard the horses snorting and stamping, and went to see the cause of it, we being by this time at such liberty that we could have made off by night if we had been willing to abandon the horses. I found the animals very uneasy, and could not quiet them, so I brought them back where they would have human company. Even then, they continued to show signs of excitement by stamping the ground until they awakened the rest of the party from their sleep. Van der Sluys thought the fear of the animals indicated either the smell of Indians or the presence of wolves, more probably the latter.

The Connecticut men were but indifferent woodsmen in other ways besides the use of the rifle, and when Hendrick and I conferred together, as by this time we had a chance to do, we both wondered that any legal authority should send men so ill prepared into the wilderness, or that the men should be willing to go. Adams was a village carpenter, we learned, and the others small farmers of sterile land, who had been tempted by the pay to undertake the expedition. Hendrick and I had agreed that the time was near when owing to the scarcity of powder caused by the wastage done by the Connecticut men, we could take a stand with them.

Feeling sure from the action of the horses that the cause of their continued terror was the presence of wolves and not of Indians, we had the Connecticut men make a great fire, while Van der Sluys and I stood watch with our rifles cocked. Presently the increasing blaze gave us glimpses of a dark form here and there in a kind of a semicircle. Adams would no longer trust himself or his followers to do any shooting owing to our small supply of powder, but made no objection when the two of us fired a half dozen shots, not so much to destroy the wolves, (the fire being sufficient protection from them) as to serve the purpose we had in mind for the next day. Nevertheless although firing in darkness at moving objects, the next morning we found parts of the carcasses of four wolves, and the Connecticut men were easily convinced that it had been good shooting under the circumstances. Nor did we say anything to disabuse their minds of their belief that they had escaped a great peril, and might encounter it again on the following night.

❧ 21 ❧

The Way Out

THE NEXT MORNING seemed a fit time to take the stand which we had planned. We had agreed that one should speak first, while now and then the other should support his remarks. So, after we had eaten Hendrick began.

"Adams," he said, "you are the leader" which for some days in all difficulties Adams had not been, "and it is for you to say what we shall do. Where there are wolves we shall find game scarce, as it was yesterday. Even if we found game, we have not enough powder left to keep six men in food until we reach the New York settlements, not even if every bullet went to the mark, and the wolves are not after the horses again tonight."

"We might eke out on berries," I now said. "But in the lower lands the early berries are ripened and gone, and the late berries are not fit to eat yet."

This all chimed in well with Adams's own fears. On the previous day no man had as much as he could eat, and he knew himself that the powder had been wasted by himself and his followers with wild shooting and no fault of ours. He and the others saw the danger, and showed their anxiety. They had but an indifferent idea of the location of the nearest settlements and of the distance to them, and we made it clear that our powder supply would not carry us to such places as they did know the location of. Adams had nothing to offer except that we return to the Wyoming settlement for ammmunition and food, but we showed him that we had gone too far for that. After waiting long enough for every man to understand fully the situation, Hendrick said:

"There is but one way that we can take with a good chance of reaching a settlement alive with proper care. We must make for the Dutch settlers on the upper Delaware, below the New York line."

Neither the Connecticut men nor I had ever heard of this settlement, but Van der Sluys had once visited it.

Adams demurred at first, but listened as Van der Sluys went on:

"Adams, you are a man of shrewdness, and you have done the best you can to carry out your orders. It is now a question of safety for all of us, as you can see for yourself. I have friends in the Dutch settlement. When we reach there, I will provide you and your party with food and ammunition to carry you across New York, or whichever way you want to go. We will go about our business, and you have only to report that you yielded to necessity and greater numbers, which will be the truth. It is either that, or start through the wilderness without food or powder, and face starvation."

After hesitating a while, and conferring with the others, who were only too anxious to accept the way out offered by Van der Sluys. Adams consented. We changed our course, and in three days neared the habitations of the Dutchmen on the upper Delaware. Here Adams grew suspicious, fearing that in turn we should become his captor, and carry him and his party to Philadelphia. Seeing what was in his mind Hendrick said:

"Adams, we shall leave our horses and guns with you, enter the settlement, only we two, and bring back to you what you need."

This seemed satisfactory, and Hendrick and I started alone on foot. On the way he expressed a doubt, which I had already felt, whether Adams could be trusted not to attempt to recapture us when his needs were once provided for, and he still possessed our fire arms, "However," he added, "I shall take care of that."

We were made welcome, and given freely food and drink, tobacco which we had long been without, and an ample store of articles for the four Connecticut men, and after our story had been heard, and our doubts made known, eight armed men went back with us to see fair play. I said that I thought that Adams deserved a surprise if he contemplated playing any trick upon us, and suggested that the settlers conceal themselves, and make their presence known only in case of need. Some of them spoke no English, but when Hendrick had communicated the plan to them in Dutch, they laughed boisterously, and consenting, left us to approach the meeting place by way of a ravine which led to a wooded bluff with much undergrowth, overlooking the meeting place.

When we had turned over to Adams the sacks of salt, meat and flour, together with the ammunition which we had brought for them; we two stood together and apart from the others, and Van der Sluys said:

"Now, Adams, we will take our rifles and the horses, and go on our way. We have done as we promised. You have your direction and will soon reach the inhabited country."

The men who held our weapons stood back, and made no movement to deliver them up, and Adams assuming the confident tone which he had used in our first meeting said:

"Not so fast. We are four and you are two. I guess you will go with us to Connecticut."

When he had thus revealed what was on his mind we took off our hats, the signal agreed upon, and singly and by couples the eight waiting settlers sauntered out of the bushes and joined us. I have never seen a man go up and down in confidence so quickly as Adams and the others did, and now no confidence was left in them. Without more words we parted from them with no sorrow on our part, but hoping they had received a lesson in manners.

A few days afterwards on the last day of our homeward journey, and when within ten miles of home, we were overtaken by Abel Strong, mounted on a fleet horse. He said that we had been given up for lost. He rode with us a while, and then explaining that he must press onward, and saying that he would leave word at the smith's shop of our coming, he rode ahead at a fast trot. When our roads parted, Captain Van der Sluys and I exchanged farewells, hoping that we might have such another six weeks together. Afterwards, Captain Van der Sluys wrote the words of a song about the high country which we had gone through. He had a clear tenor voice, and I set the words to music for three voices, and Eunice and he and I have sung it many times together.#

#On the margin of this page was written, evidently long ago, the following: "Note by Tull., 'Looking through Richard Holt's papers, I came across the words of the song made by Captain Van der Sluys, but not the music, which has been lost. Either the writer of the song exercised some poetic license with the facts, or it might have been that there was an occasional home of a settler in the less exposed parts of the highlands or along the streams. The words of Captain Van der Sluys' song, presumably in his own hand writing are these:

The Pennsylvania Highlands.
On the Pennsylvania highlands
Linger frost and snow,
While the warm airs o'er the ryelands
In the lowlands blow.
Summer is an interval,
Briefest of the year,
In the Pennsylvania highlands,
Rising tier on tier.

From the Pennsylvania highlands
Waters start and flow
To the tidal river islands
And the sea level low.
Fall the Hemlock and the Pine;
Flooded rapids leap,
In the Pennsylvania highlands,
Down the forest steep.

On the Pennsylvania highlands
Vestals tend the fires,
All the summer in the skylands,
Build the hearth-smoke spires.
Robins bold defy the cold,
When the North winds blow

From the Pennsylvania highlands
O'er the lands below.

In the Pennsylvania highlands
Men are sturdiest;
In the rare air of the dry lands
Maidens are the best.
Ruddy youths and maidens mate,
And where e'er they roam,
It's the Pennsylvania highlands
In the heart is home.

From the Pennsylvania highlands
Sons and sires go down,
Some to far lands; some to nigh lands,
Or the great port town.
Some rode forth beneath the flag;
Some would ride again,
From the Pennsylvania highlands,
At the call for men.

While the sun was still two hours high, I reached home, where the boys were hanging on the road fence, watching for my approach. Mercy Spare had given us up, but Eunice had not given us up. I was to have returned for the hay harvest. Even the wheat harvest was long past, and it was near the beginning of August.

There was no real change in Eunice, yet I felt a return of that backwardness which had formerly come over me when she would merely come down the stairs clad in a gown different from the one worn when she went to her room. But in the gladness shown at my return, and the eagerness to have me tell the story of our adventures, this feeling soon passed away. I was as eager to hear the home news as the Spares were to hear my story, and we sat up late. I asked John Spare what had been done with Jerry, and heard a tale more strange to me than anything that I had to tell. Mercy Spare and Eunice thought he could not tell the tale without their help, so they broke in upon him when he was too slow to please them, or checked him if he went too fast, and advised him when they thought he was not doing full justice to some particular part of the story. Finally, he withdrew to the background and let his sister go forward with the chronicle.

"It was Saturday night," she began, "when Jerry was captured, and you started for the wild lands on Monday morning. It was"—here Eunice interrupted:

"Gracious me, Aunt Mercy! Richard knows all about that. Begin with what he doesn't know!"

"You tell it then," her aunt replied.

"Aunt Mercy, do go on," Eunice urged.

"Well, as I said, you left on Monday. After he had some sleep, Parsons—"

"No, Sister Mercy, not Parsons but Jackson. Parsons had been after Moses Doane, not after Jerry."

"I meant Jackson. After Jackson had slept awhile on Monday, he went to search Bane's tavern. William Barnes told us that he had passed the tavern on the Friday night before and saw nobody about. Anyhow when Parsons—I mean Jackson—went there on Monday afternoon everything was shut up tight. The belief now is that Jerry played false to the Doanes in the hope of making himself safe, and that after his capture he made a confession to Jackson of what had gone on at the tavern, expecting that thus he would go free. But Bane had fled. The woman who had lived there was gone. It has come out that Moses Doane would inform Jerry when a man with money was coming that way, and Bane and Jerry were to rob the man while he was asleep at the tavern. Some of the victims parted with their money readily, not suspecting the landlord and went on their way, accepting life as it comes. But two cattle dealers—" "Three, not two," said John Spare. Eunice sided with her father, declaring it was not a matter to be made light of.

"Some say two, some three. Whether there were two or three in all, it was one at a time. You tell the rest, John."

So her brother carried the tale forward.

"These cattle dealers were travelled men, and one at one

time, and another at another, undertook to hold Bane responsible
for the loss of his money. They went so far that Bane took
to murder to hide theft. Three of these cattle dealers, all known
to have money, were seen at Bane's tavern and were never seen
again. Then it fell to Jackson to try to find out what Banes
had done with them. Here Jerry, it seems, helped him no further,
for Jackson sounded the whole house, and the cellar, and had
the hay moved in the barn, and the grain moved from the bins,
in order to see that nothing was covered up. He even looked
down the well, but the bucket had water in it, and was still
damp on the outside; showing it had been in constant use."

Samuel Pearson, who with others was helping Jackson in
the search, told me that Jackson now seemed nonplussed. He
searched all around again. At last in the tavern yard he noticed
a place where the grass was of a little different color from the
long deep green grass surrounding it. The spot was circular
in shape. Taking a pick Jackson uncovered a shallow well, abandoned so long before that people had forgotten it, and in the
bottom with only a little water about them were the two or
three human skeletons—whichever it was—and one had a twisted
leg by which, and other marks it was indentified."

"Do people think that Moses Doane had aught to do with
the murders?" I asked.

"No, they think he did nothing but to plan robbery, and
left everything beyond to Banes and Jerry, who maybe were
clumsy, and not shrewd as Doane would have been, and being
cornered, it may be, went further than they had intended to
go."

"And what have they done with Jerry?" I asked.

"Jerry is in gaol, and likely to hang."

"And, O! Richard," cried Eunice, "We are so glad to have
you back, we have forgotten to give you a message that came
for you three weeks ago. Henry Boileau brought it. As he was
passing through Germantown, the printer asked him to carry
you word to stop the next time you went to the city."

Very likely, I thought, he knows somebody who needs the

services of a surveyor, and I was pleased to think that my work was coming into demand. Doubtless he had heard of my going to the wild lands with Captain Van der Sluys. I would make sure to stop at the printer's. We talked until midnight, now about some adventures in the high lands, and now about the church, or the neighbors, until Mercy Spare said we had talked enough for tonight.

Eunice objected, saying, "I was never more awake in my life Aunt Mercy. Besides I shall soon be twenty-three years old."

"Let us see, Eunice, when is your birthday?" her father asked.

"Now, father! You have not forgotten again! On the fifteenth of September. If I must, I must, so Goodnight, Father," and she kissed him.

"Good night, Richard," and she held her hand out to me, as I got upon my feet, as Captain Van der Sluys always did when women entered or left the room, no matter how often.

✿ 22 ✿

A Recovery

A WEEK afterwards I went to the city market with John Spare, and found all our old customers back again. The Widow Stevens of Fourth Street playfully asked me to take off my hat that she might be sure that I had not lost my scalp to the Indians. We had sold everything before noon, and on our way homewards stopped at the printer's. He looked up from his work when I entered, and shaking hands, said without more ado:

"Well, young man, your chest is come, I have it here."

Had he said that some potentate in China had died and left me a fortune I could hardly have been more surprised. I had expected to hear him speak of surveying needed to be done. I had come to America in the year 1774. It was now the summer of 1779. Five years had gone by. The war with England was still going on. How could my chest come from England when commerce between the countries had ceased? There is a mistake, I thought. It cannot be my chest, and so I said to the printer. "Come and see," he answered, and led me to an apartment where the chest was. The color was dimmed; the wood was dented; the corners battered. But it was the shape and size of mine, and there were the trick hasps and hidden lock.

"How came this chest at such a time?" I asked, too doubtful to be convinced at once by what I saw.

"It came," the printer said, "on a vessel from Rotterdam three weeks ago. In the ship's papers was some kind of a record of its travels. Sent to America after you, by mistake it was carried back to Bristol and put off there, and lost sight of. The war began, and some honest fellow had it shipped to Holland to be transferred to a boat coming to Philadelphia. At Rotterdam some honest Dutchman thought there had been a mistake, and it went back to Bristol. Again it was shipped to Holland, and here at last it is."

When I heard the tale of the chest's wanderings, I was convinced. Besides everything that could be seen, the iron work, the bands, the fastenings, the wood itself where the paint had been worn off, became each moment as I looked more familiar.

"I suppose now that you have it, it will come handy to store things in" the printer said. "The clothing will be musty from the damp air of the ports and the long voyages. English clothing is too heavy for our climate, and you would not use it much if it were in sound condition."

"True," I answered, "I do not see much value in the clothing. There was some food in it, too. It would have less use now than the clothing."

I was thankful beyond words to the printer, but I could not bring myself yet to speak of what else I had placed in the chest that the dampness of sea ports and long voyages would not deprive of its value, if only it were still there. Moth and rust alone would not have corrupted my treasure, but curious men might have made way with it.

We placed the chest in the market waggon, and drove homeward, not stopping at the barn as we usually did, but driving all the way to the house. The women came out to obtain an understanding why this was done, it being out of the customary order of things, and Mercy Spare said to her niece:

"Your father has brought something from the city for the house. I hope it is the table I wanted."

"What have you brought, Father?" Eunice called.

By this time we were drawing the heavy chest from the rear of the waggon, and they could now see it, and were very curious. Presently, when we had gained breath after carrying the chest into the house, we told them, and they waited while I went to my room to search for the key. Some little while it took to find this, as wherever I had put it for safety the women had moved it. It had thus made more journeys back and forth across my room than the chest had made across the seas, and now for some time I had lost track of the key altogether. In my impatience I forgot my manners, some of them lately learned from Captain Van der Sluys, and called from the head of the stairs to know if anyone had seen the key. Mercy Spare came to the foot of the stairs and asked,

"Was it that large rusty key that used to hang on a nail over your mantel?"

"Yes. Yes that is the one."

"I remember seeing it a year ago last April. The carpenter wanted a key to open the corn crib lock, and I gave him that key; I don't know what became of it."

"Richard, there is a box of old keys on the floor of the cupboard in the outside kitchen, back in the corner."

So I went to look, and by a miracle, I thought, the key was there. Now I had to oil the hasps and the lock of the chest, for all was much rusted, and we had to wait for the oil to find its way about. With patience at last I got the chest opened, while John Spare and his sister and daughter, and the two boys looked on, interested in the mystery of the hasps and the lock. When the lid was opened the boys wanted me to close it again, and fasten the hasps and locks that they might see if they could open them, but I hardly heard them in my impatience to get at the bottom of things. Much of the clothing was in a sad state, being mildewed and rotten. Some of it in the middle of the chest seemed little harmed. I had put in the chest several parcels of dried and salted meat, and a jar of pickles for use in case of scurvy. The meat was as hard as the bone, but the pickles, Mercy Spare, who tasted them from curiosity, declared had kept well. At last I came to the bottom, and the women thinking there was nothing more to see, turned away to the pile of spoiled garments on the floor.

"Richard, you can do nothing but burn most of these things," Mercy Spare said.

Her voice sounded to me as the voice of someone at a distance.

Again I took the oil and worked at a rusted fastening in the bottom of the chest,

"What is that Richard?" Eunice asked, bending over and peering into the chest, while the others gathered close around me. The bottom came up from the edge, and there was my store of gold coins, as I had packed them away. I had wrapped each coin to prevent rubbing, and the wrappings were frayed. I took off the covers one by one, and stacked the gold on a stout table, counting the coins as I transferred each piece from the chest to its pile. Nothing was missing, and in all there were nearly 400 pounds. When John and Mercy Spare fairly understood that this wealth was all mine, they were as rejoiced as if the windfall had come to one of themselves.

"It is almost like a windfall," said Mercy Spare, "Who would think that after being lost all this time your treasure would come to you?"

But Eunice said nothing, "Aren't you glad, Eunice?" I asked.

"I don't know, Richard. It is very wonderful. None of us knew of your wealth, and I am not used to it yet. If it takes you away from us, I shall not be glad."

"Eunice, if your father will give us his blessing, we will buy old Jacob Moores' farm, for a home for you and me, and we will go to it together, but not far away."

Mercy Spare cried a little at the thought, and John Spare said he was heartily glad for both of us. He cautioned the boys not to talk about what was in the chest. As they were more curious about the hasps and lock than the contents, and were given the key to try what they could do towards opening the lid when it was closed again, they were not likely to reveal the presence in the house of so much gold.

So, I became that new owner of Jacob Moores' farm, about whose unknown identity I had speculated, and of whose good fortune I had been envious. I surveyed the farm, and found there were nearly 400 acres, and drew the deed which was signed by Jacob Moores' heirs, and so from a Redemptioner I had become a land owner. It was a good purchase, for owing to the times, and the scarcity of gold, I was able to buy at a low price for hard money, giving a mortgage for part of the purchase sum. This left me in funds with which to buy stock and implements, and such furniture as was needed after John Spare had sent over a good store. His sister, Mercy, gave to Eunice all manner of quilts, counterpaines, sheets and other things, enough I said to supply a houseful. She had them from her Mother, when in her youth she, herself, expected to wed. She never told us why the match was broken off. Nor did we know who it was that she had been on the point of wedding. John Spare doubtless knew, but he was a silent man concerning the business of other people.

Our wedding took place in the church a week before Eunice's twenty-third birthday. I thought that nearly everybody we knew was there, though I could not recollect having seen them distinctly, and after the short marriage service we drove to Eunice's old home, which had been my home for so long a time, and the road was filled with carriages and riders following us. At the house we stood up to welcome the wedding guests, and Eunice's old friends, including David Wilkinson, kissed her and wished her happiness, and told me that I was a lucky man, which I already know.

There was a great feast spread and home-made wine of many kinds, elderberry, gooseberry, cherry and some I have forgotten. Everybody drank to the health of the bride, and to the health of the bridegroom. I was called on to get on my feet and make a speech, and not knowing what I said I tried to thank them. Eunice withdrew to change her gown, and when she had come down stairs again we drove away to our own home, followed by shouts of good wishes and a great cheer. Two nights later there was a great din under our bedroom windows.

"Richard, what is that great noise?" Eunice said starting up in fear. I knew it for the noise of the horse fiddle, a box filled with stones and scraped by a fence rail. There followed a great blowing of dinner horns, loud groaning of many male voices and noises of other kinds. I told Eunice it was A Callithumpian Serenade, and that I had prepared for it. Going to the window

I called out to the men that I would invite them in in a few minutes, which I did, and served them with apple brandy and corn whiskey to drink, according to the custom, and they soon departed with good humour. We thought now that everything had happened for a time, and were ready to welcome a period of quietness and comfort in our new home.

❧ 23 ❧

Guy Ingraham's Will

MERCY SPARE had said that Eunice's birthday on September the fifteenth must be celebrated by our coming to supper at her girlhood home. We were to be through with all necessary work as soon as might be, and giving a promise for the next day to what was left undone, come as early as we could. The day before, a messenger came from Judge Morris, bidding John Spare and Eunice and me go to see him on the fifteenth about a matter of importance, to make an early start, and take dinner at Morris Hall. For all our desire for a quiet life for a time, so many unexpected things had happened to us, both good and ill, that we were prepared in a way for something new. When the messenger had gone, Eunice said to me:

"You remember, Richard, what father said about the maid who was to hear something on her twenty-third birthday and not a moment before. But it was a maid who was to learn the secret, and now I have a dear husband, and am maiden no longer, I hope we shall learn nothing sorrowful when we are so happy."

"I hope not, indeed, Eunice," I said. "We shall soon know what the secret is, if there be any."

We made our plans and all three, in John Spare's large vehicle drawn by the pair which Eunice had so often driven to the choir practicing, started on our way to Judge Morris's, Mercy Spare calling to us to be sure to be back by supper time. Eunice asked her father no questions as to the object of our visit, and her father gave no hint of what might be forthcoming, but from our silence on the ride it was clear that two of us were thinking, or wondering about what we should hear.

Judge Morris welcomed us cheerfully and I took hope from his manner. He had aged much since I had last seen him, and his eye had lost something of its former keeness. It was pleasing to me to witness his gallantry towards Eunice, treating her as if she had been a great dame who was still but a girl, albeit she was a wife. He took us into his library, and when chairs had been placed, said to his black servant:

"That will do, Pompey, you can go now, and close the door behind you. Wait—fetch glasses and a pitcher of water. Let the bucket down deep."

When Pompey had brought the water and glasses, and had gone again with his master's eye upon him to see that he closed the door, the old man said:

"I have sent for you to inform you, Eunice and Richard, of something of importance. Your father knows what it is. It has been understood between us that when the proper time came, I was to inform Eunice. Now that she has taken a husband, it is right that Richard should hear too. Eunice, do you remember Guy Ingraham well?"

Before she could reply, he continued, "John, how old was Eunice when Ingraham died?"

"Ingraham died thirteen years ago last May. Eunice was nearly ten."

"You remember him, Eunice," Judge Morris repeated.

"I have a picture in my mind of a tall, dark man, who seemed always sad, playing at the game of draughts with father in the corner of the living room at home. Somehow I can hardly think of him as out in the open—always in the shadow and he, himself, almost a shade."

"Do you remember anything he ever said to you?"

"It is a long while ago, Judge Morris, and I was a little girl. I remember that he was very gentle, and I noticed that he did not talk out as other men did, or Aunt Mercy, and I felt sorry because he seemed so sad. I can see myself, almost as if it were another little girl, standing at his knee as he played at the game, and he would hold my hand or stroke my hair, and sometimes, while waiting for father to play, he would turn towards me and smile, and I wished that he would smile oftener, and not be so sad. I have often heard father say that he was his dearest friend, and often at our house, coming on Saturdays, and staying until Sunday evening, and he must have talked with me about childish things, and listened to my chatter, and walked about; but I always see him as the sad, dark man, sitting in the shadow at the draught board, for whom I felt sorry—I did not know why—but what he said I cannot remember. I wish I could."

When she had done, Judge Morris went on;

"Eunice and Richard! Guy Ingraham and your father—John Spare has a son now, Richard—Guy Ingraham and your father were young men together at the time, almost the only time, when real friendships, such as call for sacrifices on their altars, and find them freely offered, can be formed. Such a friendship was theirs, and each made his sacrifice to it. Guy came to America from England, as you did, Richard, but he was better off as to worldly goods than you were when you landed. Guy was always a little homesick. I do not believe you are. Once John Spare saved Guy's life when an Indian, crazy with drink, would have murdered him. Both fell in love with the same maiden—your mother, Eunice, who died when you were born. Guy married a frail woman and they had one child. The mother faded away after a few years. The daughter lived to be five or six years old, a bright, pretty child, when she too died. Guy was never a strong man, even in his youth. The Indian would have made short work of him, if it had not been for John Spare. His losses broke his spirit, and with a sick man's fancy he laid his misfortunes to America. The deaths of your mother and his own wife and daughter drew Guy to your father again, and his only pleasure seemed to be his visits to your father's house."

"About fifteen years ago Guy Ingraham knew that his own time to go was near. He made a peculiar will, of which I knew nothing until after his death, and the will was accompanied by a sealed letter to me. In the will he left to me outright his considerable fortune, amounting to four thousand pounds. The will was duly proven, and I have the funds invested with Willing, the merchant, a most honest man, who has increased them. The letter which Guy left to be delivered to me after his death I will now read to you.

Great Valley, November 3d, 1765.

Respected Friend,

In writing this letter, which will not reach you until I am gone, I am aware that I am asking much of you, and that you might wish to avoid the trouble and responsibility. I am an ill man, and a lonely one, and I know not where else to turn or whom else to confide in. Mindful of our long acquaintance, and of my confidence in you and in your experience, I hope in this you will find forgiveness if I have laid too heavy a burden upon you. Owing to the state of my health it has been needful that I make arrangements for the disposal of my estate. I have no kin in this country, and none in England closer than a second cousin, with whom I never had acquaintance. Whether he be alive or not I know not, but if he were it would not alter my purpose.

I have made a will which will enable you to carry out my intentions, and bestow my fortune upon the person or persons indicated in this letter, but not named in the will. I have not consulted you because I did not wish to give you the chance to refuse.

All my property real and personal, the will leaves to you outright in order that you may readily comply with this my last wish in regard to it, which is that when Eunice Spare, the dear child of my much-loved friend, John Spare, and his wife, who is long deceased, whom in my youth I loved, attains the age of twenty-three years, if she be then single, or if she be married with her father's consent, if he be alive at the time of her marriage, or with your approval if her father be dead, my whole estate be made over to her as her own. Should she marry without the approval of her father, or of you, in case her father be dead, my wish is that my estate, when she has attained the age of twenty–three, be placed in the hands of trustees, to pay the income to her during her life, the principal to go to her issue upon her death. Should she die unmarried, or childless after marriage without such approval as I have indicated, and her father survive her, the income to go to John Spare during his life, and upon his death, the principal to go to your son, Theodore Morris.

Wishing Eunice Spare to grow up without the knowledge of this wealth, and that she may be spared the pursuit of fortune hunters, it is my wish that only John Spare and yourself know of this letter, unless it be necessary for you to guard against the uncertainty of your own life. If you think it wisest to do that, take such steps as may be necessary.

Your friend
Guy Ingraham

When Judge Morris had laid the letter down and taken off his spectacles he said:

"When the property came to me under the will it amounted, as I said, to about four thousand pounds. Most of it has been invested with my good friend, Willing, the city merchant, and it now amounts to something like five thousand pounds. There have been losses as well as profits, and for the past four years or more it has been wiser to guard the principal and not risk the attempt of an increase."

My first thought as I listened to the letter, was that Judge Morris greatly enjoyed reading it, and he looked at us now with frank curiosity. I was glad that it was not I who might be expected to speak first, for I should have found it hard to say anything that would not sound foolish. Judge Morris clearly was waiting for somebody to speak, but for a space of time not a word was said. Then it was Eunice who said:

"Judge Morris, that was a long letter, and if I understand, it lets out a prodigious secret, which you and father have been keeping these many years. Father, I don't see how you did it. I don't understand everything in the letter, and it will have to be explained to me. But I thought it meant that the sad, dark man that my memory scarcely holds, left his fortune to me, and you say, Judge Morris, that there is five thousand pounds."

"It is yours, Eunice, provided you married with your father's consent, and that you have now reached your twenty-third birthday. I must be assured of that. If you married without your father's consent, you have only the income for life. Did she marry with your full consent, John? If so, you must give me a writing to that effect. As you, John, might have an interest in the fortune if she married without it, there will be no room for suspicion that you have given a false certificate."

He gave Eunice a quizzical look as he concluded. John Spare thereupon sat down at the Judge's desk and taking a quill wrote the following at Judge Morris's dictation:

September 15th, 1779.

This certifies that on September 8th, 1779, my daughter, Eunice, was married to Richard Holt with my full and free consent. I further certify that she was born on the Fifteenth day of September in the year of Our Lord, One thousand seven hundred and fifty-six.

John Spare

After John Spare had signed the paper, he read its contents aloud. "That will do, Eunice. The fortune is yours," Judge Morris said. "Here is a deed to you from me for the only real Estate, a house on Fourth Street near Pine, which is well–rented to a widow named Stevens."

"Why," I exclaimed, "she is the widow who would have none but Eunice's butter, when our customers left us because of the Doanes."

"Yes, Richard," John Spare said, "Eunice will never be able to ask from her a higher rent."

"Now, young people," Judge Morris went on, addressing Eunice and me, "Your father knows that Guy Ingraham's letter surprised me more than any letter I ever received in my life except one, and that was a letter which I found on yonder desk, and it was written by Moses Doane. When I learned, afterwards, that some of the English officers had also mistaken Doane for Lord Pelham, I was not as crestfallen as I was when I came downstairs in the early morning, and learned that my guest was not Lord Pelham, but a clever highwayman. I had let out something of your secret to Doane the day before, nothing about the fortune, nothing definite, but just enough to make him aware that your father and I knew something about you, Eunice, which we were concealing. I had better tell it all to you or you won't understand.

"You see, Eunice, Guy Ingraham had placed me in a delicate position. My son, Theodore, might come to a share of your fortune, or to sole possession of it in two ways, one by marrying you, and the other under the letter to me. It was not likely that all those things would happen which would have to take place before the property would go to Theodore, but they might do so. With your fortune in my possession, I would turn myself into one of the fortune hunters that Guy tried to guard you against, if I encouraged Theodore's attention to you."

My eyes were off and on turned upon Eunice to see how she was bearing up through all these complications, centering about her. Very modestly and becomingly... had she borne herself, and now I saw the color mounting to her face. She had never spoken to me about Theodore's proposal of marriage to her, nor had I told her of her Aunt Mercy's communication to me.

The Judge went on:

"I could not encourage such attentions honorably, and I tried to discourage them. Perhaps you thought me cold towards you. Perhaps you wondered why. Now you understand."

Eunice could keep quiet no longer.

"Judge Morris," she said, "after Father and Richard, when I knew nothing of this fortune, I admired you beyond any man I ever saw, and now I love you, not as I do them. That would not be right, but in a different way almost as much."

The old man arose from his chair, hobbled over to her, and taking her hand, bent over and touched it with his lips.

"I am not quite done my confession yet," he said. "When I thought that Doane was Lord Pelham—I knew what Theodore was about when he was riding off to church so often, just to see you—I told him there was a reason why he should not marry you, without telling him what the reason was. Theodore had gone to the city to enter the British army, and when I unfolded myself to Doane, I thought I was enlisting the help of Lord Pelham—a much older man than Theodore, a man of rank to whom Theodore would listen—in weaning away the boy's growing affection for you. Richard knows that Doane tried to make profit out of your father, through what he gained from me. Your father came to see me and I told him just how much, and how little Doane had learned, so he was not disturbed about that end of it any more than I was.

"Now that is about all. Here is your deed, which I now make delivery of to you. My accounts with my friend Willing are all transferred today from my name to that of Eunice Holt. Richard you will have to help her take care of her money. It has been easily come by. It can be made to go as easily. If you want advice come to me."

"Judge Morris, how is Theodore?" Eunice asked, and I heard a note of sympathy in her voice.

"Very well, and hard at his law studies in the city. He plans to go to London to study at the Middle Temple, after he is grounded here."

We were all silent for a few minutes, the Judge very cheerful, looking as if he were used to bestowing fortunes every day in the week, John Spare, self contained as always, and Eunice as sober as I felt. Then Eunice spoke up:

"Judge Morris, I do not know how to thank you for the care and trouble you have had and for your thought of me. I wish the sad, dark man of my memory could know how you have fulfilled his purpose, and how you stood between me and your own son, in order that I might be guarded against even the semblance of a fortune hunter. Theodore was no fortune hunter. He never heard of any fortune. Nevertheless, I think it was very fine of you, Judge Morris, and I know that Richard thinks so too. I am coming on so that I can tell what he thinks without his speaking, and we shall never forget it, or cease to thank you in our hearts. How strange it is! I am afraid I am not quite myself, Guy Ingraham! I wish that he could know."

"Perhaps he does, my dear", said her father. "Perhaps he knows."

There was a knock on the door, and Pompey opened it to announce that dinner was ready. The Judge led Eunice to the table and placed her at his right. John Spare sat opposite the host, and I on the other side from Eunice. Two black men waited upon us, and again the health of bride and groom was drunk, this time in Madeira, upon the Judge's proposal. After Eunice had withdrawn, we three men sat for some time at the table, Judge Morris giving me a sober talk about the care of Eunice's money. He thought that with the over stock of paper money, every day more worthless, and the interruption to business caused by the war, that commercial investments would be risky for a long time to come, but that land was now cheap, and it would be well to draw the money from Mr. Willing and buy land.

An hour after dinner we said farewell, and Mercy Spare was relieved to see us drive up the lane in time for the supper, which she had prepared.

"Bless me," she exclaimed, "you have all grown sober again."

We told her that the great secret was out, and what it was, and I cannot say that the birthday supper was a very merry one. John Spare, alone, was quite himself, and took a turn at rallying us on our lapses into silence, but he had the advantage of the rest of us in knowing the secret for many years. We tried vainly to be casual in talk, but attempted persiflage died stillborn, and Mercy Spare said that a fortune was almost as bad as the Doanes.

Conclusion

ALL the secrets were out. Eunice said that she hoped we would never have another secret, but in course of time she had one to whisper to me, and when our boy was born, his mother named him Guy after the sad, dark man of her childhood's memory. Our Guy was fair with blue eyes, and not sad at all, but merry.

As time went on, I had more and more surveying to do. The long war was over, and men began to take heart and reach out. In my business of surveying, I learned where the best lands were in the market, and following Judge Morris's advice, we bought before the prices advanced. We had a grist mill, a fulling mill and a saw mill, besides the farm and timber lands. The city grew rapidly, and there was a good market for everything.

Now and again, Captain Van der Sluys, who grew in prominence and became Sheriff of the new county to the westward, visited us, and often after young Guy was sound asleep Eunice and Hendrick and I sang the song which he had written, but when he and I talked of making another journey together to the highlands, Eunice threatened that she would sing the song no more if we said aught about it.

Long before this, before we were fairly settled down in our home, Jerry's trial came off, but Bane, the tavern keeper, had fled; Moses Doane was dead; outlawry had ceased, and Jerry got off with imprisonment. Moses Doane at last had been caught off his guard, and was shot down, some of his pursuers regretting it, saying that there was some good in him. Others of his family met with a like fate. Joseph Doane went to Canada. Twenty years afterwards, he returned to make a visit to his former home. The past was forgiven and a number of persons, who had at one time sought his life, talked with him in all friendliness about the old times, and there was a better understanding of former differences. I asked him what had become of Joey Doane, and was told that he was doing well, west of the Susquehanna.

Theodore Morris became a great lawyer in the city, and we came to trust in him as we had confided in his father up to the time of his death. John and Mercy Spare live on making much of family anniversaries and holidays, which we spend with them. Eunice and I continued to sing in the choir, and one of the first things Eunice did with her money for the good of others was to carry out a plan which she thought of, and perfected all by herself. She talked with David Wilkinson about it, who welcomed it heartily, and with the Rector to win his approval, and then employed a singing teacher from the city to come to the church every Saturday afternoon to instruct the boys and girls of the countryside in singing music at sight, and in the singing of the chants and hymns used in our church service. This instruction was given at no cost to the pupils, the only condition being that such as should be chosen because of the excellence of their voices were to sing with the choir at the church services. The result, in a year's time, was so fine that numbers of persons, not members of the church, came to hear our church music, and we were all proud of what was done at Christmas and Easter. After it was well under way, David Wilkinson continued the work very successfully until he grew too old, by which time our Guy was able to take his place.

With no particular merit of my own, except that I have tried to be faithful, I rose from the position of a Redemptioner. My master became a second father to me. Some would now call me a landed proprietor. I know three other men who started in America in the life of a Redemptioner, as I did. Each of them married his master's daughter, as I did. All prospered, as I have prospered, though none of them has a wife so gentle, so sweet, so fair, so capable as Eunice. So, I think it is not the condition of a man's start that matters greatly. When I last wrote to my brother, Robert, in England, I said that I thanked the good God who had guided me to America, and I hoped the next year, with my dear wife, Eunice, to visit him in my boyhood's home.

ACKNOWLEDGMENTS

Grateful acknowledgment is made to Miss Charlotte Pennypacker who furnished the manuscript written by her father and to Isaac Rusling Pennypacker's two nephews, Joseph Whitaker Pennypacker and James Anderson Pennypacker, who have overseen the conversion of the manuscript to its current book form.